Sinking Bell

...

Sinking Bell

▪▪▪ *Stories* ▪▪▪

Bojan Louis

Graywolf Press

Stories in this collection appeared originally in different form in the following publications:

"Make No Sound to Wake" in *Ecotone*
"Volcano" in *Numéro Cinq*
"Usefulness" in *Off the Path Volume II: An Anthology of 21st Century American Indian and Indigenous Writers*
"Trickster Myths" in *Yellow Medicine Review*
"As the Meaningless as the Origin" in *Alaska Quarterly Review*

This publication is made possible, in part, by the voters of Minnesota through a Minnesota State Arts Board Operating Support grant, thanks to a legislative appropriation from the arts and cultural heritage fund. Significant support has also been provided by the McKnight Foundation, the Lannan Foundation, the Amazon Literary Partnership, and other generous contributions from foundations, corporations, and individuals. To these organizations and individuals we offer our heartfelt thanks.

Published by Graywolf Press
212 Third Avenue North, Suite 485
Minneapolis, Minnesota 55401

www.graywolfpress.org

Published in the United States of America

ISBN 978-1-64445-203-5 (paperback)
ISBN 978-1-64445-186-1 (ebook)

2 4 6 8 9 7 5 3 1
First Graywolf Printing, 2022

Library of Congress Control Number: 2022930740

Cover design: Adam Bohannon
Cover image: John McFlanagan
Spine image: Andrew Bayda

For Sara and Billie Dólii

Coolness—
the sound of the bell
as it leaves the bell.
    —*Yosa Buson*

Contents

Sinking Bell

Trickster Myths

My stomach sank gradually, as if escaping, toward my asshole.

While I leaned against the rough spackled wall of a hotel afterhours, I watched off-work girls and hundo-flashing shitheads from the Two Points Cabaret imbibe and flirt. Caught slight smiles from a few girls who walked past me to the bathroom, none whom I knew beyond the winks they gave me after I threw dollars on stage or tucked twenties into their G-strings. The shitheads I didn't bother with, we were the males, and our energies were meant for the girls. Our attention on one another usually ended with puffing up and a lot of shit-talk.

The girls were attractive, intimidating sexually—drawing everyone's attention to their bodies—but my thoughts were on my mother, uncomfortably enough. She'd been bitten nearly a month before by a rabid dog while visiting clients in Phoenix who had yet to claim their relocation benefits. As a result, she would have to stick herself in the stomach with syringes full of expensive medicine twice a month for as long as she lived. She never let on to anyone that the shit in those hypodermics made her sick. When I went to my parents' for dinner, my dad, sister, and I observed as her weight dropped, her energy faded; bled-out pale, she looked archaic, like ash in the wind.

But my presence at the hotel soiree wasn't a distraction from the disquietude I felt about my mother's health so much as it was anticipation of Bella's arrival. There were three levels to this after-hours, and I imagined how Bella and I might navigate them. In the third-floor room, the party, she and I, of course, would socialize, I'd meet some of her coworkers, a guy or two, and hopefully we'd nudge one another toward the door. That was the ideal scenario, but as on most evenings I spent with her, I'd have to wait until she got her sociable fill. In the second-floor room, a dealer up from Phoenix slung smoke, pharmies, and coke—grub-thick rails lined out on stomachs, thighs, and cleavage. I'd sworn off blow and pills, though if I had been seduced to relapse, I'd have snorted or ingested anything off Bella's beautiful body. In the first-floor room, some girls tricked. Whether they worked at the Two Points or had appeared from elsewhere, I had no idea. Here my imagination stalled, added to my anxiety that Bella might be there, go there, or have been there during some other party, maybe blowing a guy or, more disturbing, letting him enter her. It was paranoia, a controlling tendency of my gender that interpreted her sexual freedom as troubling, though what I imagined taking place in the first-floor room wasn't at all freedom but a fate passed down through a desperate play of power. And my problem was that I'd begun to want more of, or maybe it was more out of, Bella.

■ ■ ■

Sometime after my anxiousness turned to indigestion, she entered the room and bullshitted immediately with two other peelers, wearing puffed-sleeved midriff tops and skintight jeans cut low, exposing ass-cleavage. The three lit pastel-colored cigarettes, belted mandarin orange vodka from a bottle clutched by one of the ass-crack girls, and rested their arms on one another's shoulders, creating a barrier of private merriment. Their white skin and sure sway reminded me of the delicate chalk of aspen saplings blown through a forest of bark-tough, drab pines.

I watched Bella's lips—soft, made more appealing by a film of flavored gloss—move with words I couldn't hear but imagined were meant for me. She was a girl I could kiss for hours, the want of her mouth softly wetting its way across my body, me desperate to return the gesture.

Releasing one another, the girls filed across the room, tapping shoulders, leaving a wake of hungry, critical glances. The two friends passed me without lifting their heads, but as Bella approached, she paused, touched me just below the collarbone with her small fingertips, and I stayed put. She entered the bathroom and closed the door.

Ten minutes passed, but it could have been thirty, before the girls emerged finally—flush-faced, eyes widened, hands smoothing undernourished stomachs. Rather than being annoyed or impatient, I was reinvigorated, ready for the night to blur to dawn. The two other girls returned to the mix of the room and Bella winked goodbye, moved to a corner, and sat on the floor. I followed her down. She held one of my hands, her skin unlike skin—cold hardness, but brittle, somehow breakable—she felt beyond my grasp. I imagined my hands gliding up the length of her thighs toward the denser parts of her body. The crevasse her hips made when her legs were pushed up. Pulling out, the run of my come like a flash flood–filled creek.

We stared at each other, made small by the room's cacophony. Her coke-blown pupils were black mouths, the oxidized green of her irises the lipstick that gave those noiseless hollows endless depth—speech lacking tongue. I was weighted to the floor and looked at her gray lambswool sweater, which molded her breasts and slender body, her worn jeans downplaying her sexiness and elegance.

She let her chin drop, took me in from beneath her eyebrows.

"I didn't like what you gave me," she said. "You shouldn't write the typical boy-angry-over-a-girl type of shit. It doesn't get you laid, first of all, and girls are much more mature than any infatuated boy's hang-ups. So what you gave me was obvious, see-through."

I'd given her some piece about a Navajo guy in his early twenties who knocks a White girl up, breaks her nose after she decides to abort the fetus without his consent, and gets thrown into county. To my knowledge, I'd never gotten any girl pregnant, hadn't ever hit one. Bella was right, though—misogynistic, falsely masculine, unattractively immature—the pages had a beginning and an end, a catalyst, but they weren't about anything. They were a reflection of life, disappointing and boring.

"It's not about me," I said. "Guy I went to high school with did that or something close to it."

Which made her view of me worse, now I was cowardly, couldn't own up to the truth she relayed to me.

Bella sighed, surveyed the crowded room behind her, and turned to me, brushed some imaginary ash or lint off my pants, a signal that the night wasn't a complete loss if I could somehow make myself attractive and interesting again.

■ ■ ■

Our first real interaction had been weighted with a similar awk-
ward silence, at least on my part. We'd both joined a weekly
writing group that met in the heavily incensed and third-world-
textile-hung living room of a literature PhD student. With his
MFA background, he had started a free writing workshop for us
troubled souls who were either on probation, in therapy or recovery, or simply had a desire to heal ourselves of some emotional affliction. There were six of us, Bella and I included.

A few weeks in, I worked up the guts to approach Bella and
engage her in conversation, rather than continuing to meet her
eyes for a second and mumble hello as we passed each other in
and out of the workshop. I wanted to commiserate with her, com-
plain about the four other sad sacks who'd tricked themselves
into believing that what they were writing was actually heal-
ing them instead of traumatizing them over and over again—
the PhD guy didn't know how to respond to what we wrote with
anything more than "That was moving," "So powerful," "Yes,
let it free," "You all convey such beauty through such pain," or
some other similarly vapid, pathetic shit. I had convinced myself that Bella and I would find commonality, but she didn't so
easily offer criticisms of the other workshop participants.

On the evening I first finally spoke to Bella, she was smoking on the curb in front of the PhD guy's house with the slightly
older girl, in her late twenties, who was seeking to recover herself
after a breakup with an abusive man she'd almost married. She
and Bella seemed bonded by their apathy toward men. I stood a
short distance off, puffed on a cheap unfiltered cigarette, which I
thought made me less commercial, less prone to being asked for
a smoke, and watched as Bella and the sagely poetic, older girl
shared a cigarette and talked. When Bella stood to return to the
workshop, she stretched her arms above her head and arched

her back. This, of course, aroused me, and my courage waned, nearly failed. The thought of my attraction reminded me that other guys also found her form enticing, which inspired two thoughts: one that if I botched my introduction, then the other guys most definitely did, too, which didn't comfort me; and the other that if I didn't approach her, I'd be nothing more than a brooding, substance-abusing, chain-smoking Navajo metalhead who yearned to express his tortured identity. I didn't want Bella to know who or what I was, only how I thought.

As I approached, Bella and the other girl quieted, glancing quickly at each other. No words in mind, I blabbered about Bella's piece in which a cocktail waitress discovers an unconscious child next to a Dumpster and takes it in, only to have mysterious kidnappers show up to threaten both the girl's and the child's life, until the two flee the desert metropolis for a college town in the mountains.

I asked a vacuous question: If one saw emptiness in another person, did they in fact see, or come to see, emptiness within themselves? Bella and the other girl considered this, seriously, I thought, before Bella bent over laughing and the other girl covered her mouth, looked away. I fumed, considered cowering off to beat myself over the head behind a bush. But I stood my ground and laughed nervously with them at first, then let it all go.

Bella said, "All I can tell you is that to fill a hole is to begin a pile."

I attended the workshop two more times, until an incident where an *ese* kid on probation spit on the PhD guy, called him an ignorant, White minority-lover, and stormed out all pinche, pinche and puto, puto. The rest of us sat as the guy cried and expressed his pain about not ever being truly appreciated, no matter the generosity of his intentions. I don't think anyone listened. We were there for our own bullshit. When the guy finally did get a hold of himself, someone told him to focus on school, not on anyone else's pain. On the way out, I asked Bella for her number, as I knew I'd never go back.

■ ■ ■

Below the noise of the party and through the silence that had settled between us, Bella took my hand, rubbed her slender thumb along the nicks and scars from teeth, drywall, and asphalt shingles. The juxtaposition of her smooth, pale hand with mine cautioned that she'd not be hurt by me, that I'd fade from *her* memory, and I envisioned her standing in the entrance to a room where I sat in the center, the hallway behind her unlit, her head turned in profile as the door was closed by someone unseen.

She broke the moment by asking how my mother was, if she was still sick or getting better. It disconcerted me when Bella asked about my life, though I'd always surrender some bit of information. Perhaps it was self-doubt about addiction and rehab or my front as some badass not prone to violence but not one to run from it. She once asked why the people I wrote about possessed aversions to or affinities for pills. It was easy to see what she was getting at, what anybody would be getting at with that question. The answer was simple: before the writing group began, I'd been three weeks out of a one-month rehab, was still trying to make sense of the situation. Bella didn't press me for more and I didn't offer it. If I did, maybe I'd have more of the time I desired with her, meaning I'd spend more than one or two nights a week with her. I wanted to ingest her physically and intellectually but knew it was impossible.

"She's better," I said, "but still sick. The doctors she's seen keep prescribing treatments, but they all make her ill. She hardly says more than that she's not feeling well, and we never ask. My family, I mean."

"You think it has something to do with all those coyotes and skunks being rabid?" Bella asked. "Maybe they're biting dogs, or vice versa, and the dogs are getting infected, moving it up the food chain rather than down?"

I had no idea, didn't dismiss the possibility, since reports were growing of pets being infected with rabies through encounters with skunks or coyotes. I felt odd, more disconnected, discussing this with Bella. I'd played my mother's initial illness on her the first time we hooked up, some sympathy fuck, rather than just being myself. She'd come over with half a fifth and I'd wondered where, with whom, she'd been—the kind of thinking that drives a guy crazy, turns an easygoing relationship into a volatile thing, where possession becomes the absolute. We drank, talked authors, passion, risk, sex, and the importance of climax in order for people to feel calm around each other. She said she was glad we were friends, which made me panic, the word *friends* a boundary around my image of our intimacy. I inhaled her smoke-and-peppermint scent, told her about the dog bite, my mom, rabies, my worry, and we kissed, found ways in under our clothes. Before she took me into the silence of her, she told me we didn't have to be friends. We didn't have to be anything. I ran my teeth across the length of her shoulders and collarbones, along the muscles in her neck, and came inside her because it felt like escape and I knew she took care of herself.

■ ■ ■

Tired of straining to hear each other through the party's whir, we moved off the floor, made our way outside, and stood next to the walkway railing. We commented on how fresh the air was. Blew our smoke into it. I left the conversation about my mother with her potential for getting better. We returned to stories. Bella was thinking she'd write one about all the rabid skunks and coyotes, some metaphor for human blight, perhaps even a zombie thing, but dismissed it immediately as overdone.

She asked, "Don't you guys, I mean Navajos, place a lot of *belief* in the coyote, the trickster?"

"Sort of," I said. "It's not *belief*. He's not a god or anything. Coyote is just someone we tell stories about, moral and creation tales. His chaotic behavior brings harmony, whether he has an adventure, comes to a realization or epiphany, or gets beaten to a pulp and dies. I mean, it shouldn't get all the useless attention it does, as if it were the whole basis of our culture and not just an element."

Bella nodded. Her brow and frown concentrated.

I told her that as a child I'd heard stories from my parents and grandma about coyote being a pain in the ass for the holy people, the deities; rearranging constellations, seducing humans, losing limbs, dying, resurrecting. She'd read as much in an anthology of Native American trickster myths, which I assumed had been edited by some Indian-loving academic, and she admitted doubting the guy's credentials.

We talked rabies and infection, about some of the reports we'd heard. Coyotes and skunks shot, put down. Hikers coming across the carcasses of either two coyotes, a coyote and a skunk, two skunks, even a medium-sized dog and a coyote positioned in what looked like a death match. We talked about a zombie coyote. A mysterious infection and outbreak, sickness beyond mend, the improbability of his smooth regeneration; every mishap, any death, causing him to wake uncured of a growing frenzy; violence foaming from his jaws, transparent boils rising out of his fur; he'd skulk, malnourished, yellowed nails clicking against concrete, black and brown teeth shattered in his mouth.

Bella imagined gelatinous matter in his eye sockets instead of eyeballs, and his ability to track her despite his lack of vision. It would scare the fucking shit out of her. *Looking into a void and it looking back.* She mentioned Lovecraft and a couple other horror guys, but I'd never read Lovecraft or any horror of the sort.

Our conversation ended there and we stood next to each other, content in our own thoughts. I wanted to put my arm around her, pull her close by her hip—touch her, but I was too distracted to feign suave. Instead, I thought back to an interaction with my mom. I couldn't tell if she was feeling well or not, since she keeps her words short and has even been called stoic by people who are unable—too stupid, really—to think or imagine beyond that stereotype of Navajos or any other Natives in general.

I'd been sitting at the kitchen counter. My dad and sister were out. My mom cooked while I alternated reading the shitty local arts paper and *The Iliad*. She never pried beyond asking how I was doing whenever I answered that I was fine. She tricked it out of me, made me think I was fooling her by talking around the question, but she saw through me. I was her son.

"How's everything going?" she asked. "How have you been since, you know?"

The only thing either one of my parents had said about my stint in rehab was that they loved me, were somewhat disappointed, and asked that I promise never to end up there again, which I did—promise never to, I mean. I told her it was nothing I couldn't handle, but in truth I doubted my ability to fake being happy and struggled to be content. I mentioned the workshop, described it as some new form of expressive therapy, and lied that I was still going and that it would get me through everything. She looked at me sideways, nodded.

"Meet anyone interesting? A girl, maybe?"

Navajos, especially old-head Navajos, view wealth and happiness in terms of family size—children, grandchildren. It always seemed to me that to be, or end up, alone was a circumstance deemed impoverished, destitute. My parents had only me and my sister, neither one of us with any obvious potential to produce grandchildren other than by accident. My sister didn't have a love interest, and what I had with Bella wasn't or didn't feel like love, though love doesn't always denote children.

Yeah, I told her, there was. She suggested I talk to this girl, get to know her, be certain she had strong values, a good upbringing, parents who weren't dysfunctional or divorced. A lot, I thought, to expect to check off if I were to bring home Bella, or any girl. She thought Bella a strange name for a White girl, asked if her parents were hippies or drug addicts, and when she said the words *drug addicts* her voice faded and we said nothing for a moment.

I said I didn't know Bella too well. Intelligent, strong writer, very attractive, a girl I wanted to know more about. Truth was that she wasn't good enough for my mother's moral compass and I wasn't confident I'd be able to accept or love her despite my mother's judgments. It wasn't Bella's life that was faulty. It was mine, with its structured expectations.

■ ■ ■

I can't say what drove me to pills, don't discuss it, and feel I'll never be cured or *healthy*, but will survive, maintain, as long as I'm able to stave off the drowning feeling of failure or inability.

Bella had cashed her blow earlier, in the bathroom with the girls, and wanted to hit up the second floor. Bored with the party, she'd score a gram or two and head home. We descended the steps at the far end of the walkway, doubled back on the second level to a room at the opposite end. Bella knocked three times, someone pulled the door open—this entrance, our exit.

Bella knew the dealer, which didn't surprise me. He was a rhinestone-studded-shirt-and-jeans-wearing thug named Silvo, who'd removed all the regular bulbs from the lamps and replaced them with red ones. The effect was skeevy: bar, nightclub, fucking cabaret. They hugged, which unnerved me, but then most girls usually hugged guys, rarely shook their hands. They talked business, all this was. Two grams—if Bella stayed, did a little in the room, he'd charge her for only one. Silvo cracked large, hairy knuckles, his gaudy gold rings clicked together, and he licked his lips. Bella considered the offer, looked at me, not for permission but to see if I'd stay or turn and leave. I sat on the edge of the still-made queen bed, she in the chair next to a small table. The crimson light altered the hue of her skin, made it look like she had a fake tan. I felt distanced, the sudden alteration of her appearance made me consider what it meant to have her, not in sexual terms, but to have her like one's ability to access a person on a whim and know they'll be there whatever the day, hour, or circumstance. She could have me that way. But in this light, it was all unreal.

Anytime I watched Bella dance onstage, I felt insubstantial. Seated beneath her, I felt that I gazed down and not up at her, as if I'd left my body to observe the two of us in that atmosphere. The cabaret lighting never altered her complexion in any way;

the lights made her more defined, more present. We'd sleep to-gether after her shift—being inside her like being deaf, sealed in a room; the hum of our fucking enhancing our senses—she not sweating as much as me. Every time I pushed into her, she bit my chest and shoulders in response, and that pain helped me last, frustrated me, made me grip her wrists too tightly, which she thought necessary for us to see each other.

"What if we pay for two grams?" I asked Silvo. "What then?"

"Now we're talking," he said. "Homeboy knows what's up. You'll get the third gratis, no problem."

I wasn't holding enough ends. Bella covered the rest, winked at my unprepared offer.

The first rail slid bitter down my throat, straight to my heart, catapulted to my brain, tripping synapses. The second coagu-lated in my nostril. I dabbed saliva up my nose with my pinkie to aid the drip. I continued snorting and dabbing through the free gram and the next. Neck and chest hardened, palms dried like they might dust away, the only thing that quenched my thirst were Bella's thighs. Each time I groped her, she guided me off, allowed only sips. She wasn't annoyed, embarrassed, or self-conscious. She was satiated with the coke—I wasn't needed.

Our time in the room ended when Silvo declared he was out, out of what he wanted to give us, any more and we'd have to pay, take it somewhere else. It was after three or four, more customers would arrive soon. Bella had less than a gram left. I asked her to go with me to a cash machine so I could score more for later, this gesture, the acceptance of our similar fates.

She smiled, exaggerated, and touched my face, guided a kiss to my cheek.

"Well, let's fucking go," she said.

■ ■ ■

In the passenger seat's flip-down mirror, Bella applied lip gloss and I reached out, stroked the length of her hair, the play of browns and copper like petrified minerals. We'd come down from the second floor, passed the first-floor trick room, and I'd asked her if she'd ever known anyone, a friend, perhaps, who'd been in there, and if so, what was it like?

She stopped, turned to me, and said, "You don't really care if anyone I knew went in there. You only care if I have." Her pupils dilated, contracted to pinholes, and dilated again.

"Have you?" I asked; the coke urged me on.

Bella cringed, the question an affront to her character, of course, and to what we might or might not have had together.

"I don't do that," she said. "It's all in your head. It's in every guy's head. You think that because girls like me make money off guys like you, guys too fucking cowardly to date a girl, no matter what the fuck she does for work or money. You just want to know how many other dicks I've sucked. Well, how many pussies have you licked, asshole? I've never judged you about that."

Any response I might have conjured up would have made no sense. I couldn't hide the fact that I was curious, worried about it, that it would, in the end, have made a difference.

There was a mundane inevitability to our destinies, one akin to the coke coursing through our bodies. The high would end no matter how much more we snorted. We'd be left panicked, joints aching, the brightness of the following day making the potential of our together*ness* no longer possible. We'd need the darkness of our own rooms to recover.

We exited the hotel parking lot without speaking. The headlights cast light across bark-beetle-infested ponderosas. I couldn't help think that this whole town was sick. We pulled up to a convenience store, decided that both of us were too fucked up to go in and operate the ATM, and agreed that a bank with a drive-up cash machine was a better option. No one to see the bug-eyes loose in our heads.

Back on the main road through town, Bella, quick and in a monotone, said, "Let's do a bump. You want a bump?"

I did, if only to rebuild the broken connection between us.

She removed the tiny bag, flicked it against her palm, kneaded it with her fingers, rolled up a twenty, and pulled a quick snort from the bag. She offered to lean over and hold the wheel so I could concentrate on getting a good bump. We nearly hit the curb but she righted the car in time, and I took a bigger hit than I wanted. I grabbed Bella on the crease of her thigh where I liked, told her I wanted her, and she told me, "Fuck you, you can't just fuck me," and slapped my hand away. It'd have to be something more, if there'd be anything at all.

"I mean, I think, I want us to be something more," I said.

"That's not what I meant," she said. "You don't understand."

I didn't know what I was supposed to understand, maybe it was the coke, or how she always disarmed me, but I was out of responses.

"It's okay," she said. "It's not something you need to worry about now."

We turned onto the street where there was a bank and spotted a coyote trotting ahead of us, thirty feet, maybe. We whispered "Holy shit" at the same time, looked at each other, relieved somehow that this utterance had brought us back together. The manifestation of our earlier conversation directly in front of us. Bella suggested I cut the headlights and follow the coyote slowly. I decelerated, idled closer, and the coyote turned around once and continued forward. Bella watched it intently, fidgeting with her hands.

"Why isn't he running away?" she asked. "You'd think since we're this close, he'd run away."

"Maybe he's rabid. I don't think they are cautious of what they're supposed to be cautious of when they're rabid."

Bella gulped, said, "Will he attack, then? What should we do? You think we should kill him?" And after considering a moment: "I think we should kill him, with the truck."

She tapped the dashboard like some commander at battle.

Bella had a point. We couldn't make a call to pest control or the Forest Service. It was late. The last thing we needed was for some cop or animal service to be patrolling anywhere near us.

We double-checked that our seat belts were buckled and looked across the cab, lit dimly by the streetlights, and into each other's dilated eyes. We weren't ourselves and didn't know it. Our outlines were blurred beyond the fault of our vision. I accelerated, hardly reached twenty miles per hour, and the coyote made no effort to run. I knew we'd struck it by the way it bumped beneath the tire and jolted the steering wheel.

We idled on quietly until Bella said, "Let's check if it's dead. I don't think it should suffer."

The coyote looked smaller lying on the pavement than it had when it trotted ahead of us in the truck's headlights. I couldn't help but think it was a pup lost from the pack or one bold enough to scout out alone. Either way, it had encountered me and Bella. Its hindquarters and stomach had been crushed by the front tire. The semi-digested contents of its intestines spilled out alongside it. Bella retched a few times before she seemed to regain control.

"Is it dead?" she asked. "Please tell me it's dead."

I knelt close to the coyote's head, its open eyes shuddering in fear, death throes. Foam ringed its mouth. It didn't breathe, but its eyes kept moving.

"It's not dead all the way, I think."

Bella yelled "Fuck," asked what we'd done, and paced from where the coyote lay to the sidewalk. Her regret and confusion compelled me to comfort her, to make this seem right. I walked to her, took her by the shoulders, pulled her to me, and she relaxed.

"If you want to wait in the truck," I said, "I'll take care of this."

She stepped away. "I don't need you to be all, *Girl, wait over there while I handle this*. I'm fine where I'm at. Here, I'll get you a fucking rock."

Bella ran toward a ring of river rocks around an aspen in front of the bank. She lifted and weighed a few before she brought me a fairly heavy one. I imagined the plop and thunk it'd make if thrown into the deep pool of a creek. I took it over to the coyote, made a couple of mock motions of how I'd throw it down, then threw it as hard as I could, wary of missing and crushing my toes.

I vomited when the coyote's skull crunched and blood splashed out onto my shoes. After I wiped my mouth, Bella gave my arm a reassuring squeeze and walked back to the vehicle. I looked to the coyote's head, there was nothing left. It had to be dead.

∎ ∎ ∎

We ditched the thought of buying more blow and agreed on a drink at Bella's.

In the parking lot of her apartment complex, we maintained the silence that had started after I'd crushed the coyote's skull. I was embarrassed that I'd puked, self-conscious that my breath permeated the truck and that I had chain-smoked the entire drive to Bella's place.

Finally, she said, "I don't know that I have anything to drink, but you can still come in."

It was fine, I told her, it didn't make any difference, I just wanted to be far from the coyote, or what was left of it, and certainly wasn't in the mood for other fucked-up people in denial of the coming sun. There was nothing to say, nothing to do but get out of the truck and into Bella's apartment. Neither of us made a move to open our doors until Bella removed what little blow she had left. One bump at best.

"I'll split it with you," she said.

I told her no, she could have it, but she insisted. It'd take the edge off what had occurred earlier. We portioned it out onto a CD case. Bella went first. After I killed the bag, I gathered the residue left on the case with my finger, rubbed it into my gums. This simple process calmed me. Bella gathered the dust in the bag, rubbed her gums.

"Don't you have any music?" she asked.

I recognized this hesitation to enter her apartment as an effect of what we'd just done together, an irrational action that we believed would quell our fears or what we thought were our fears. Hers: my eventual rejection of her and her lifestyle, this one more night of *This might be the last night*. Mine: my relapse and staying with her despite expectations or traditions. We'd placed all this upon what we'd heard and created, destroyed it without cause or provocation. And there we sat, waiting for the other to acknowledge any of this.

I grabbed another CD from the door pocket, and rather than be the one to make this and previous moments mean more, I got out of the truck and smoked a cigarette, told Bella that if she wanted to sit and listen to the music, I'd smoke outside on her side of the truck. She shrugged and I felt the tension between us loosen to annoyance, to the courteous time one takes before releasing the other. I didn't tell Bella how I felt or what I wanted, only another story I'd heard.

It was told to me by an uncle or maybe my dad, certainly not my mom, because she never told me anything like this, a story about the skunk and the coyote that goes back hundreds of years, where the skunk and the coyote were at odds, if that was always the case isn't important, but they were at odds with each other over food and survival and how to prepare food, and one of them, the skunk or the coyote, thought cooking it on a spit was best, fastest, while the other thought cooking it underground wrapped in yucca leaves was better, the meat more tender, candy off the bone, so they both decided to give it a go, the only thing was that cooking it underground did take longer, they would have to take shifts watching the fire, so the skunk said he'd go first, coyote could rest until the skunk woke him for his shift, so while coyote slept the skunk prepared and buried the food, kindled and lit the fire, until it was the coyote's turn to eagerly feed the fire, drool at every spark, every added log, until he woke the skunk and slept, dreaming of what he'd soon devour, but when he woke of his own accord and with a rumbling stomach, all he saw was a pile of bones, which grew as the skunk tossed them down from the cliff where they cooked, the skunk laughing and telling the coyote he should have been smarter, the meat was so good, so tender, it was almost impossible not to finish it all, and the coyote, half-starved and too weak to climb the cliff, could only suck the marrow from the bones to maintain himself and not starve to death.

Bella rolled the window up, slid out of the truck, and stood before me.

"You think that's what we're doing, then? Feeding off of one another? Then which one of us is getting only the bones?"

She hugged me. The warmth of her body reminded me it was cold, the sky bruised with the first hues of dawn. I wanted to be inside with her, at rest and in recovery, before I left for my own place, where I thought I would shower and change, perform the basic tasks to start another day. Then—and I imagined all this— calling the number the rehab clinic had given me and making an appointment for counseling, some objective third party to talk to, and showing my face at the address of a Narcotics Anonymous meeting they gave me. I'd stashed the address and number in a book I'd already read. The words and pages a summons for a memory, like the skunk-and-coyote tale, that might remind me of a better time with misremembered people.

I held Bella, kissed her a few times, followed her lead. We undressed ourselves in her bedroom like a couple long together. Our lips touching soft pulses of throats, blunted horns of elbows, and tender lumps between belly buttons, pelvic bones. We fucked slowly, and when we were done, the sun shining hard through the blinds, we slept, wondering what we would each come up with in order to leave the other first.

Make No Sound to Wake

Evening gusts moved shadows and air the dogs couldn't smell. This late into Niłch'ih Tsoh, with the ground buried beneath three days' snow, two mutts curled for warmth inside a scrap-wood shelter built against the northeast side of a hogan. Travel this night was unlikely though not impossible, if someone were forced to venture across the darkness and cold.

Many generations ago this land had belonged to Hastiin Łįį'dóó ł'izhé, a pious if not saintly man, quick to judge those of us living in imbalance, out of tune with the harmonious songs of the earth and constellations. Who had come to own the property I had no way of knowing.

Inside, the hogan was furnished meagerly, several bedrolls with a blanket each, two wooden chests, a loom, a metal wood-burning stove in the center, and a washbasin with shelves for food and dish storage. A couple of saddles were piled near the eastward-facing door, though I had seen no corral anywhere near on my approach.

In the dim light of two lanterns, a scrawny-shouldered boy played a game of mimicking an older girl. He wore a shirt a few years too big for him, the darkened skin from being winter-fed circling his eyes. The girl crouched with her skirt flared around her, dirt caking the cracks of her rough-skinned hands.

"Your face is dirty," she said. "Wipe it off."

"No," said the boy, "you wipe yours off. I don't like it looking at me. It's ugly."

"You're the ugly one, an ugly dirt boy."

The girl sprang forward, lumbered toddler-like on her knees, and tackled the boy. Their skinny bodies fell flat against each other in the fashion of a man and a woman bedding together. Any sort of play like this between kids in my day was taboo. It was disrespectful, overly sexual, and unbecoming of children who would become adults.

A woman, face chiseled and hair grayed, busied herself at the washbasin, her back turned toward the children. Near the bedrolls an old wind-beaten woman hunched over a blanket folded on her lap. She yelled, "Yaa'dilah," and paused her game of seven cards set in a row, stacked according to number, color, and suit. A game I didn't recognize, but then so much was unfamiliar to me in those days.

"Doo beehaz'áa da. You kids don't act that way. Nia, get off your cousin."

The kids continued to wrestle despite the old woman's urging. Punishment would have been my next impulse, had these delinquents been mine. Especially for the boy—it's boys who grow into irresponsible men with hungry hands, groping eyes, and temporary hearts.

The old woman's cards scattered as she rose. Grabbing the

girl by her ponytail, she yanked her off the boy, who scampered backward to the south wall.

"You're hurting me, shimá sání," the girl whined.

She was slapped, let go. The girl sat still only a moment before fake-stepping toward the boy, who flinched. She was slapped again, shoved to the floor. Angered, the girl glared at the boy from her defeated position.

"Flincher diigis," she said.

"You're stupid," whispered the boy, huddled against the wall.

The grandma retrieved her blanket and cards, rearranged them, and resumed her game.

Ignored or forgotten, the children, like alert prairie dogs sniffing an unfamiliar wind, stood and chased each other around the stove at the hogan's center. The girl galloped ahead of the boy, taunted him with whinnies as his failed grasps caught the empty space between them. He dove for her and missed, tumbled toward a corner table and into the legs of the younger woman, slicing onions for the mutton stew simmering on the stovetop. She cut her thumb and cursed. Blood seeped into the fine crevices of the halved onion so it looked like a bloodshot eye. She loomed over the boy, knife in hand, slammed it flat against the cutting board, the blade twanging and falling silent.

It was obvious this was the boy's mother. Her patience for disciplining him was measured—she directed his attention to the physical pain he caused her, allowed him to know it wasn't the flow of her blood that hurt her, but his continual refusal to stay seated quietly, to listen.

"Nia," she said, not looking away from her son, "clean your cousin's face. It's dirty."

"But . . . ," protested the girl.

"I told you. Clean his dirty face."

Nia took the boy's hand silently, led him to a washbasin half-filled with filmy water, wet a rag, and began gently, or reluctantly, to wipe his face. The mother shouted that Nia was only smearing the dirt and so she scrubbed harder, until the boy's face reddened from her effort. She smoothed his thin black hair, dabbing his face with the cloth.

"It'll be okay, Grayson," she said. "It was an accident. You didn't mean to hurt your mom."

"Don't you call him Grayson," said the mother. "He's no man's son. Just a boy. A gray boy."

The girl, turned defiant against the mother's dismissiveness of the boy, uttered under her breath that he'd always be Grayson to her. The mother glared at the girl, the crowfeet at the edges of her eyes deepened, and her mouth opened like a cow's. Before she could yell at the children, the grandmother told her not to waste her time and youth chastising them, she would only wrinkle faster, turn her hair white.

"You just finish making dinner. I'll settle the kids down."

Returning to her chopping, the mother said, "That's what you were supposed to be doing."

The grandmother waved off the comment, motioned for the glum children to sit at her feet.

This was how winter was spent: stories told to teach, kids playing the moccasin or stick game, not running about wildly—though in my day all this had begun to change too.

A somber quiet settled within the hogan, and the old woman began a story. She had been a girl when she heard it, hardly older than the boy, though better fed. The story was about a woman driven mad who had killed her children by locking them inside their hogan during winter, where they starved to death and froze together as a solid, misshapen hunk of ice. When spring arrived, their hardened bodies thawed, and the woman cooked and ate them. Some years later, after the woman had died from the grief of devouring her children, she began to haunt the frozen nights in search of misbehaving children, whom she would freeze and then consume during warmer weather.

The boy sat horrified. The girl seemed to feign indifference and doubt, but I could see the small wavering of her eyes. The boy turned ashen. His fear pushing him down into the thin veil of his shirt.

The timing of the grandma's story wasn't right, however. There was no way the old woman was a girl when I'd been alive. It wasn't even possible for her mother to have been alive. Perhaps the old woman's grandmother was a girl then? It's difficult to say. The only things true about the story were that I had existed and then had ceased to.

▪ ▪ ▪

My memories occur in no particular order but all at once, happening continually, in imbalance and disharmony.

My parents and I had lived in Łeejin Haagééd, which was half a day's walk from the cliffs overlooking Hałchíítah—the color of dusk skies in summer and beyond, on the western horizon, the blue peaks of Dook'o'oosłííd.

We had been forced from this place by the Bilagáana and their Bi'éé Łichíí'í. We were allowed to return, after years in exile, to a barren landscape and a dilapidated hogan, looted but fortunately not burned. My father was surprised to find the two windows intact. Our home had been used, probably, as a safe haven for vagrants or those journeying to some better place.

My parents had returned to die in their home and not in exile, though I'd returned to live.

I was one of the few adolescents to survive the many days' march to Hwéeldi, where we were given rations of bland white dust, pungent brown grounds, and dirty water. Aside from enduring the deplorable conditions, we were forced to live with an enemy band of Naashgalí dine'é. We stole from one another and often fought, until we learned that our real enemies were the Bi'éé Łichíí'í guarding us, as well as the Nóóda'í, who were allowed to raid our prison while the soldiers stood by whooping, laughing. It was during these years that I was raped, first by a Nóóda'í, and then by a lanky Bilagáana soldier, who kept his cowardly blue eyes shut and called me by some other name. I wanted the pale soldier to look at me, to see me, starved and weak, a bony girl without breasts or hips. I wanted him to know that his strength over me was pathetic.

Before we were marched at gunpoint to Hwéeldi, the Bi'éé Łichíí'í slaughtered our livestock, left the carcasses to rot in the sun, and set our crops ablaze, the dark smoke invading the clear expanse of sky. This was the fate of every family across Diné Bikéyah. Some families fought and were killed, their bodies stripped and burned. Others fled and were captured. If not bound, beaten, and marched, they were murdered. The girls and women were raped multiple times before their energy and lives left them. Those able to escape hid in the maze of canyons at Tséyi', did their best to preserve what little of their livestock remained—eating only the old and weak, breeding the young—and foraged piñons, wild onions, and corn from abandoned gardens.

My father died young, not too long after we were released and had returned home. I was a young woman by then, pregnant with another child of violence. Before he died, my father praised our leaders for negotiating a treaty that allowed us to come home, and that offered him a small amount of peace and solace, though he wasted away during the season of our return. My sister didn't make it as far as my father. She coughed blood until it killed her. We buried her beneath a tree somewhere between Tóniłts'ílí, our home, and Tsoodził. I don't remember when, exactly, but certainly it was before we left that prison, before my brothers were taken to schools far in the East, well beyond Sis Najiní and Hwéeldi, even. The Bilagáana thought the absence of men would cause the people to fall into disarray and chaos, to depreciate and succumb to the weakness they saw in the women from their world. They knew nothing beyond their hatred for us. They didn't know that our women did everything men could. Women held the power the Bilagáana are so obsessed with. I never saw my brothers again, there was no way to learn of their fate.

My mother worked herself to death keeping me alive. During her final years, she began to forget me. She no longer recognized what few possessions we owned or where we lived. Looking across the landscape, barren except for sand, she asked if she was able to go out and play with friends who didn't live too far off. She'd be home by sunset, she said. What heart-broke me most was waking one morning to find her more lost in her mind, building an invisible fire and stripping naked for a nonexistent ceremony, covering herself in invisible ash.

My grandparents had been lucky. They had escaped into the canyons along with the first wave of people who avoided capture. Of those refugees, many were never heard from again. No one knew if they had perished, hidden in the canyons, or if they had later emerged and disappeared into unfamiliar landscapes.

I knew my grandparents wished to die on Diné Bikéyah, where the Diyiin wanted them to be, where we all, at some point, should be.

■ ■ ■

What the grandma got right in the retelling of my story was my lack of a husband and the scrawniness of my two kids, the bulbs of their spines nearly bursting through their skin whenever they bent over. My spirit faded with every thin meal I was able to give them. I was unfamiliar with the work of storing food, herding sheep, and weaving. In truth, I was never taught how to farm, butcher, or make a loom like most women. The old woman's tale shed no light on the dim corners of my life, the secrets I hid from my kids, or the darkness I made of myself.

Imprisonment, violence, and witnessing my family die taught me to dance men away from their families temporarily. My slender, hardened body didn't disgust them. All Diné changed in this way, as if nearing death had sucked the skin closer to our bones. We imagined a healthy softness through the desperate need of our knobby bodies closing together. Not a lot of us, it seemed, were looking for forever, though perhaps we should have been.

I also gambled, was good at it. Won jewelry, sometimes livestock, most anything people were willing to surrender—except children, because they can be burdens disguised as gifts. I took this style of life and it took me. The weak men, angered by losing, attacked and beat me at times. One unlucky bastard tried to rape me, but my life had seen enough of that, and I took the deer-antler-handled knife I'd won off him and cut his neck down to the spine, swallowed the blood that poured down on me, to get the strength to get back home to my children. It didn't sicken me, only intensified the bitter taste of my own blood in my mouth. Weeks and months after this, I was called the murderous-whore-witch, and even now, generations later, I'm thought of in this way. It's how I'm bound to this earth.

And so the old woman continued her version of the story of how my children and I met our deaths. One abnormally long and snowy winter, I abandoned them yet again to go to a Ye'ii bicheii some unreasonable distance away. My intentions for going I don't remember exactly, though I could surmise that it was to obtain supplies, seek the false hope of help. A blizzard arrived, the landscape was buried, frozen. The children had hardly any wood, just as little to eat. The trip should have taken three, maybe four days. But I never returned.

"Those kids," the old woman continued, "didn't have any wood, any food, so they burned their hair first, then their clothes. They began to eat the walls. The woman, far away and unable to reach her children, begged hand-tremblers and crystal-gazers for help. None would, except for a witch who lived in incest with her only son. Those two lived off the suffering and spirits of others. The witch offered the woman help if she promised to give all she owned, which the woman did. She was stripped, covered in an ash mixed with the crushed bones of bodies stolen from graves. The witch told the woman the mixture would keep the cold off her, she wouldn't feel a thing. The witch sang on the woman, and the son took the woman's breath into his body and exhaled it into his mother's so the woman's soul would never find its home and would be forever lost."

My children were discovered frozen, stuck to the empty stove, their hair and fingernails gone. The people who found my kids refused to touch the bodies, feared they'd break apart and release spirits that would haunt them. Spring arrived and my children seeped back into the earth, the earth where I walk the nights, wailing out names I don't remember.

I embrace the children I find. They succumb to the cold of me.

"The woman, like the witch, seeks souls to sustain her. And so she returned to her children and devoured them." The silly old woman howled out a few times and cackled, set the children crying and seeking the comfort of her skirt. As if I'd howl in such an obscene way. She hurried away from the kids toward the stove, took a small shovel and scooped some ash out, and smudged an arc on each child's forehead. This appeared to calm them, though they looked at each other with furrowed, uncertain brows. The girl, eyes widened in realization, removed a small pouch beaded at the edge of its opening, pinched some tá'dídíín, and placed it on her tongue, then the boy's. They closed their eyes and prayed, possibly, for protection against a force like me.

In the months before my children passed, they stopped praying, didn't greet the sun with open arms and stare at it for a blink's time, the fire blue-glowing behind their eyelids afterward. They had given up hope that it'd get better for us, for them, really. I wouldn't ever get myself together and find a man, or anyone, to help or protect us. I never demanded that they pray. I was already a ghost to them.

The wind picked up, rattled the north window, where the mother stood slowly cleaning bowls, a cutting board, and the knife she had used in preparing the night's meal. She ignored the children, her thoughts a vast distance away. She stroked the palm and fingers of one hand. I could tell by this motion that she was waiting for someone, had someone in mind. Her face relaxed for a few moments, until the whimper and complaint of one of the children turned it stern, impatient.

"Can't you kids shut up for half a night? Nothing's out there. Don't let Grandma scare you. It's not good to be afraid, anyway. It lets everyone know you're weak."

The children apologized, offered their quietude in exchange for assurances of safety, were placated with a snack of piñons.

Behind me on the white horizon, snow crunched as a heavily bundled figure approached the hogan in long strides. The wind blew, and the mutts sprang up, barking. The figure, gruff-voiced, yelled at them to hush. He neared the door, affixing white, stringy hair to his face, put on a hat in the shape of a cone with a white ball at its top. His peculiar clothes were completely red, with what looked like white rabbit-fur trim around his pants cuffs and the bottom of his coat. He slung a coarse green sack over one shoulder. Was this stout and burly man the one who the younger woman waited for? I wondered.

The mutts continued barking.

The man knocked hard, slow, three times. Inside, the children froze with fear. The mother faced her child and niece, an expression of feigned surprise creasing her face.

"Who could that be?"

The children pleaded with her to brace the door shut, but the mother pulled it open a crack and peered out.

"Make the sound," she whispered.

"Just let me in, it's goddamn cold out here," said the figure.

"Make it or I'm not letting you in."

The figure grumbled and bellowed out, "Hoo, hoo, hoo."

The mother opened the door. Icy wind blew through everyone's hair as the man hobbled in, making the depressed-owl noises again. The children screamed. The girl dashed away from her grandmother and dove behind a pile of bedding.

The boy shouted, "It's the lady!" He ran toward his mother,

then thought better of it, since she had allowed the thing in. He retreated to his grandmother, crying, trying not to cry.

What an impossible scene, I thought: this oddly dressed man with a green sack, the mother's affection toward him, though he obviously terrified the children. Perhaps my children had felt a similar terror with each man I brought home, or during the long days I was absent, the wind or some creature thudding against the door, scratching at the window. Perhaps my children were too weak to show their fear. Or was it that they were hardened and tough? Was it with a lack of fear that they perished during that frozen winter?

The old woman was busy trying to coax the kids from their hiding places, telling them the man was harmless. He was a friend bringing gifts because it was a special day. A day the Bilagáana celebrated for children. Meanwhile, the mother readied tea for the figure who leaned against the door, his bored and deep-set eyes watching the reassuring movements of the old woman.

"No, no, no. You kids don't need to be afraid. This man is Santá. He's a gift-bringer from a pole in the North. It's Keeshmish. Keeshmish is a special day."

"Then what's the sack for?" asked Nia, peering out from her hiding place. "Is it for us? Are we going into the sack?"

Grayson was pulled by his arm from where he was hiding, behind his grandmother, and forced to face the red figure.

"It's okay, it's okay, it's okay, son," repeated the old woman.

As the children neared the plump and matted Santá, he extended an arm. A calloused hand gripping what looked to be a red-and-white-spiraled hook, which emerged from the rabbit-fur-cuffed sleeve. Its blunt tip glistened like an icicle. It was meant for the boy and he knew it. He flailed like a panicked animal held by its scruff and, once loose, ran a circle around the stove, only to be confronted by the laughing Santá bellowing "hoo, hoo, hoo" between breaths. Scurrying in the opposite direction, the boy was confronted again and again, until he collapsed, all snot bubbles and puffy-eyed wetness.

"It's just candy," the mother said, taking the hook from the end of the furred arm. "It won't hurt you. Quit being a baby and look."

Grayson watched his mother snap the hook, it hung broken in half in her hand. She picked at the straight end, removing the candy's translucent skin. She stuck it in her mouth crunching off the end, offered it to the reluctant though curious boy.

"Peppermint," she said, "it's called peppermint candy. Have some. Santá brought it for you."

The boy took the candy from his mother, who smoothed his hair once. He bit a small amount, held it in his mouth, and crunched.

"It's funny," he said. "It tastes funny." He crunched again with his mouth open, licking at the air as if it might add to the strange food's flavor.

Nia popped up from the bedding, hurried to Grayson, peered at the candy he was inspecting, and asked for her own.

The invader extracted another peppermint hook from the green sack and handed it to the girl. She turned the thing over in her hands, picked at its clear skin, and put it to her tongue. She asked the boy if he liked the thing and he shrugged, still suspicious. Each kid stood with candy in hand, staring from the hook to the red figure, back to the hook again.

"Yaadilah," said the grandmother, "they don't get it. We should have said something before. We're just freaking them out. Larry, take off that stupid beard and give them the presents."

"Who is Larry?" the girl asked.

The mother rolled her eyes, waved the children off, and poured hot tea into two mugs.

Larry removed the stringy white beard, which had been hooked around his ears, and shoved it into a pocket of his coat. He took the strange hat off, revealing greasy, thin, unkempt hair. He rubbed a hand over his reddened face, dropped the green sack to the ground, and kneeled down to extract a couple of shiny boxes, one of which he tossed toward Nia's feet and the other toward Grayson, hitting him in the chest. The two stared at the boxes on the ground before them, like disappointed and uncertain pups given scraps.

"You're supposed to open them," said the old woman. "Don't be scared. Come on, now, show me what's inside."

While the children bent down to open the boxes, I watched Larry turn his attention to the mother, pull her closer to him by the waist, and put his mouth to her hair. He whispered and she giggled, curled into his embrace. She handed him a mug to warm his hands. But it wasn't the mug he wanted. I knew this of men. It hadn't changed.

The boy watched. His fright turned to confusion, perhaps anger. He removed the glittering skin of the box, set it unopened in his lap. Looking away from his mother and the strange man, he joined in Nia's excitement as she pulled out a doll with wheat-colored hair and pinkish skin. Its blue eyes were vacant, though they seemed to follow everyone in the hogan. I wondered if the Bilgáana had themselves begun to use black magic to steal away and change our people. The leveling of land and livestock, trees resembling the deformed bones of the dead—if this violence and cruelty hadn't been enough for them.

The girl said, "This doesn't look like anyone I know. Maybe

like the boarding school teachers, only prettier." She walked the doll along the floor, mimicking the way the Bilgáana spoke. *Yada-yada-yada, yada-yada-yada.*

The old woman laughed, asked what in the world the doll was saying. The girl repeated the gibberish, to the grandma's delight.

The boy frowned, determined not to open his box. His mother noticed, but rather than comfort or help him, she turned her attention to the strange man.

"He needs to do it himself," she said. "He'll be grown before I know it, then I'll be alone."

"The sooner the better," said the man, kissing the mother's hand, holding his cup out for more tea.

My body doesn't recall the touch of affection or want, the ache of hurt or pleasure. It's transparent, as unnoticeable as unmoving air, the thin light through suspended dust.

The girl leaned against the boy, asked if he wanted help opening the box. He nodded. Before she could guide his hands through the movements, he slammed the box twice against the ground, shook it near his ear. Surprised, the adults in the hogan wondered aloud what he was doing. Wasn't he happy for the gift? The boy replied that whatever was inside, he wanted to be sure it was dead so it wouldn't attack him once set free. The mother, exasperated, turned again toward the man and urged Nia to help the boy. The kids set to opening the box, extracting what looked to be an oddly shaped wagon with no hookups for the horses. The boy struggled to hide his delight. He rolled the thing back and forth, creating shallow ruts on the dirt floor that the mother would surely wipe away.

▪ ▪ ▪

The night passed. The children played make-believe with their new toys, while the old woman made beds—males on the north, females on the south—and the two lovers sat closely on chairs, whispering, laughing.

In my home, my son had slept alone on the male side of the hogan. As I've said, I never had a man around more than a night. Even when my boy was scared because some creature howled or hurried past our door, wind shaking our windows, I'd tell him, as he pleaded with me to sleep next to me, that he should quiet, never show weakness or vulnerability, only indifference and strength. In my final absence from my children, I'm certain they didn't cry. I'm certain. They did the things that would help them survive. Sought the sustenance of the walls that contained them, and when their spirits left their bodies, even then, they didn't cry. Because of their final silence, I'll never know their sound, never remember what they looked like.

The group prepared for sleep, Larry sneaking his bedroll closer to the mother. Before the lantern was extinguished, he told Grayson he needed to get used to him coming around and staying. The boy gave no response, remained still, eyes shut against the dim light, the yammering adults, and the cold. Lost to his family in some unknown place in his imagination.

I'll never be known.

The truth about me, my children, and our deaths will never lead me toward freedom. Forever will I be a nameless fear, the epitome of coldheartedness, neglect, and failure. The ghost of a culture that values women most but never speaks the names of their dead. Not like those we fought who arrived from the south, or the Bilagáana and their Bi'éé Łichíí'í, who stormed in with bullets and fire. These people who carry the names of their dead on their hateful hearts and inflict that suffering on other people. Worship their dead with death.

The bodies surrounding Grayson heaved with sleep, their backs turned against him. The noise of those snoring hid his movements as he got out of bed and put on dungarees and a flannel shirt over his long underwear. Next his socks and boots. Dressed, he crept to where Nia slept, removed the doll she had placed next to her head, and returned to his bedding to retrieve his toy. Next to the door, he hesitated. I saw clearly the fear in his eyes. He tiptoed back to the stove, knelt next to the shovel the grandma had used earlier, and traced his name along the cold metal surface, gathering ash, which he smeared across his forehead. He collected more from the stove and covered his face.

Pulling on his coat, the boy turned the knob and eased the door open, hurried through the doorway quietly. The wind had quit, the air held a stillness, empty as stopped time. Dawn was a thread across the horizon.

The boy skittered atop the frozen snow, his breath acting as clouds for a cloudless sky. The stars were bright in their multitude, their disordered, mischievous origin. Had I had a heart, it might have raced. Raced with the boy running along the path to the outhouse, just over a hill and out of sight of the hogan. Raced against the sun opening the door for the Diyiin to pass momentarily from their world to this one, so that the old woman might pray and make her morning offering. Raced against time now and all time.

I wouldn't lose this boy. I believed, in some way, he'd felt my presence, was found.

Reaching the outhouse, the boy threw the toys into the pitch of the stinking hole. Stayed a moment to know they were gone, and turned, my boy, my baby, turned to me and I was present to him. He saw me and knew what I was. The cold came up through his coat and into his mouth, into his widened eyes. His breath became invisible, his skin turned the ashen color of his face. And before the mutts could begin barking, and before the old woman could rush to the door screaming his name, I'd taken him home, forever, with me.

Volcano

If he stayed ahead of the project manager's bullshit for the next two days, Phillip George could have the weekend to take Jared to the base of Mount Elden, where unconnected caves offered seclusion and refuge to amorous teenagers and homeless transients. Ever since there'd been a school unit about bats and the caves they inhabited, the kid had been cutting bat shapes from the delicate pages of the Bible he'd found in the dresser drawer of the weekly/monthly motel where he'd been living with Phillip since his mother, Phillip's cousin, had abandoned him there. Phillip's girlfriend, Benita Blackgoat, had protested the hike: the trip might be too long for the kid's physical and emotional capabilities, no thanks to his Down syndrome. But Phillip was intent on nothing obstructing his plans.

His shift ended after another twelve hours and a call from his project manager asking him to remember to lock the gate to the jobsite. He completed this task every day, always the last one to leave. Vick was a knew-enough-to-be-dangerous construction lackey turned PM, probably because he was the general contractor's relative or a favor owed to a friend. He arrived at jobsites in his overly chromed and small-dick lifted white Ford F-350, clean shirt tucked into ironed jeans, boots shinier than used, holding a clipboard of meaningless to-dos and a list of places where he'd eaten lunch and with whom. He was the perfect middleman between the GC and clients/investors due to his ready knowledge of available tee times and recipes for wine spritzes.

While Phillip chained and locked the gate, he imagined Vick yammering among clients and contractors about his annoying employees, the rising price of materials, and the perpetual failure of other subcontractors to meet deadlines. Shit-talk that made the workers seem like ignorant numbskulls, though most actually were. But Vick created a false sense of dignity on behalf of the workers—they might be stupid, but they worked hard to get the job done—which offered the right amount of assurance to the clients and contractors so they believed the work they were paying for was true craftsmanship instead of a project completed just good enough.

After the site was secured, Phillip rode the bus home, glared at his reflection in the opposite window, the fluorescent lights making him ashen, his negative-like image superimposed over the dated storefronts the bus rumbled past. He dozed, tried to ignore the lurch from potholes left after winter storms and the conversations crackling around him.

■ ■ ■

The dusk sun left the clouded and smoke-filled sky a flare of fire as Phillip walked across the parking lot of the Elden Motor Inn to the office. Inside the heavy glass door, he set down his tool bucket and drill bag, rang the bell like he'd done every week for the past few months.

The motel owner-manager appeared in his typical collared rayon shirt rolled to his knotty elbows, a brightly patterned tie, and tight Wranglers stretched painfully over his large and well-sat ass. Boots fashioned out of ostrich skin creaked as he positioned himself behind the front desk. He often wore a white cowboy hat, but today he appeared with black hair bushed on top of his head.

"You just missed the hura cabrón," he said. "Rolled out of here ten minutes ago."

"No shit," said Phillip. "Saw a couple cruisers from the bus on the way in. What was it? A little domestic violence, meth-heads exposing their freaky, fucked-up nature?"

"None of that, ese. Just the locotes from 1A and 2D arguing and coming to a half-assed fistfight over going halfies on the last bachita and who hotboxed it. Pinche borrachos. You'd think they die of agua or straight oxygen."

Phillip nodded. More of the same down-and-out, struggling-to-keep-one's-head-above-water bullshit. Generally meaningless and harmless, though as consistent and disheartening as shirked overtime pay. He slid $270 over to the manager, who pressed his tree-trunk-like fingers on the crinkled bills until Phillip released them so he could pocket the money. Phillip never saw him use the register or any sort of record book. The couple of times he'd asked for a receipt, the manager had simply pulled a notepad from behind the counter; written the name of the motel, the date, Phillip's name, the amount paid; and scrawled figures resembling a *T* and an *M*.

"That chica of yours not being too hard on your pockets, hombre?"

"No," said Phillip, "she's too busy keeping her head in her books and exercising. What makes you say that?"

The manager shrugged, tongued at something between his teeth, and opened his mouth to say more. Phillip palmed the counter, waited for whatever might be said next.

"Well, hombre, just before the hura got here, I found your niño playing around back, close to the basura. Nothing to stress about, I took him back to your pad. The puerta wasn't locked and your chica was laid out cold, snoring on the bed. Don't worry, ese, I didn't see her tetas o coño. She was wearing una fantástica tracksuit."

"Fucking hell," said Phillip.

The evening reds had faded, the night air was warm but cooling. Many of the other tenants had their doors open, the noise of reality television mixed with the dying traffic on Route 66. Phillip's tool bucket and drill bag banged against his numbed calves; his shoulders felt as if they'd been pulled from their sockets. The single window of his room glowed at the edges of the drawn curtains. His eyes itched, watered slightly from the ever-present smoke of the first series of controlled burns. It was still early in the fire season, but he and the rest of the mountain town hoped a substantial monsoon might dispel the previous decade of drought.

■ ■ ■

Before Phillip moved into the Elden Motor Inn, his lady, Benita, had been living in the dorms at the university, which was required of freshmen who didn't already live in town. They'd been dating a year long-distance by then. He'd been working for a large commercial electric company that landed most of its contracts with a developer that built resort hotels in and around Phoenix. A large and temporary employee pool ensured he'd have work for no fewer than six months and also the knowledge that he'd be laid off once a certain phase of the work was completed. He never saw the resorts in their final glory, never got to finish or trim out the receptacles, switches, or lighting fixtures. He only bent and secured what felt like miles of half-inch-to-two-inch conduit, pulled circuit boats to and through junction boxes, and made up and readied the wires for the eventual installation of chandeliers, sconces, dedicated circuits, and smart-dimmers. His work was invisible, necessary to get right the first time with nothing left to troubleshoot once the main power was turned on. He would hump a slow Greyhound north every other weekend to play stowaway in Benita's dorm room, flipping idly through her textbooks while she studied and he waited for sex or a meal. It felt perfect: fucking and eating, cuddling to movies in bed. They frequented house parties—five years older, he purchased and delivered the booze—where she drank skinny-something-or-others. The low calorie count allowed her to indulge in one or two, three, maybe, while Phillip sipped ginger ale and watched the throng of youthful exuberance waste away in a random student's living room. Benita counted and calculated consistently: calories, miles, reps, fat percentages, heart rates, cholesterol levels, grade point averages. She was a health solutions major with a focus somewhere in nutrition; her ambition to become a role model who battled obesity and diabetes in Navajo communities by addressing the lack of education about healthy cooking and eating. She wanted to dispel the myth of fry bread, which was a significant health hazard, due to its high calorie content. Fry bread was a remnant of colonization and forced removal, the Long Walk. All of which Phillip understood, though at the end of his long workdays, he could give a shit about it.

When Phillip entered his one-room domicile, he found Benita snoring open-mouthed on the bed, hands clasped death-like over her stomach. He grabbed her leg and shook it, her body moved limply. This incensed him and he shook her violently until she woke.

"You can't stay awake another hour to keep an eye on the kid?"

"What?" she asked drawing out the vowel. "Don't shake me like that. I'm not some wasted, passed-out 'adláanii."

He let go of her leg, removed his hoodie and T-shirt, threw both toward the clothes piled beneath the sink outside the bathroom, and attempted to pull off one of his steel-toe work boots without completely unlacing it. Once free, it nearly hit him in the face and he shouted, "Fuck," threw it against the wall, and received a muffled yell and pounding in response. While he fussed with the other boot, Benita said she'd wanted to fit in a BodyPump class before picking up Jared from after-school daycare. This was a growing tension between them. Her over-committing to Phillip's needs and agreeing to get the kid no later than five so he wouldn't risk losing overtime. There was no one he could afford to pay to watch the kid, no matter how much overtime he worked. And, anyway, who would want to babysit a nine-year-old with Down syndrome whose trust in strangers was lacking at best and who also took issue with anyone other than Phillip touching the back of his neck or ears?

"Jared was asleep. I locked the door. I thought we'd both nap until you got back. He's never wandered out alone before. It's something to pay attention to now. It won't happen again."

Benita faced him, smoothed the plushy green warm-up top fitted over her curves. Fuck his anger, he thought, and hoped she would turn away from him so he could see her from behind, approach, and press his tired body to hers, caress the firmness of her abdomen.

"Fucking shit. You know the manager found him playing in the trash around back? What if those cops from earlier found him? Deep shit. We'd be in deep shit. Hell, his mom already fucked him over. We don't need to too. Even if it's . . . because one of us fucks up."

She turned away, blamed her distraction on the stress of her final semester, the need to carve out time for self-care.

Their argument waned, and Jared, hunkered quietly beneath the round two-chair table next to the window, called out, "Hello." Strange how he became invisible, thought Phillip, despite his being what occupied his mind and energies most. Maybe that's how he had escaped earlier. His presence demanded all of one's faculties, yet he could vanish and still seem to be in all places.

"Hey, little man, I'm sorry. We didn't mean to yell so much. We're both tired."

The kid emerged from beneath the table and hugged Phillip, forcing the breath out of him. He wondered if the kid would ever become strong enough to crack his ribs.

"I'm cool, man. I'm cool, man," Jared said.

Certain Jared hadn't been in any real danger, and that the manager was a person he could count on, though he'd never make it a thing between them, Phillip reassured himself by squeezing Jared's shoulder lightly, and headed toward the bathroom.

"You need to pee or anything? Or is there some homework Benita can help you with?" he asked over his shoulder.

"I don't need to pee. Benita already helped me with my homework. I need to make more bats now."

While Jared got out scissors and the Bible, Benita sat quietly on the edge of the bed, facing the window. Rather than reengage the argument they were having, or were about to have, Phillip thanked her for helping Jared with his homework and asked if she could keep an eye on him. She acknowledged the request by looking toward Jared, who waved at her. She waved in response and turned the TV on.

In the shower, Phillip imagined his life unfolding differently. Not quitting the high school club soccer team before a couple of college scouts had taken the time to watch a few matches. Had Phillip stayed, it was likely he would have been one of the guys selected to play with a full ride to one of the state universities or, at the very least, a community college. Had he stayed, he would have gone. From there would have proceeded a life he had never fully envisioned. Pro, semi-pro? Would he have finished his degree? Would he have had a major? Construction management or hotel and restaurant management? Something that required little academic effort but that would have had the potential to make him more money than electrical work. Would he have homed in on the young Benita giving him eyes, seemingly the bad boy, though in truth he was decent enough for her. Stable, mature, and in no way related by clan, a consistent roadblock for both and potential romantic relationships. Instead, he was living check to check, with his cousin's abandoned retard and a girlfriend who would probably leave him once he got fatter, once she graduated and found her dream job. There he was, beholden to everyone else, with the soap and hot water rinsing off the grime of another fucking day and, maybe, more of *himself*.

Relieved to be clean, he slid open the shower curtain and found Benita leaning naked against the door, her clothes piled neatly in the corner. He hadn't heard her enter, so deep had he been in his own head. Her brown body was toned, evidence of her increased physical strength; her black hair lay in strands across her small breasts, covering her darker areolae. He felt himself get hard.

"You're leaving him alone again," he said.

"That's what's special about you. You never think of yourself first."

She grabbed a towel, dabbed his body, and used it to dry clumps of his wet hair. She frowned, whispered that the kid was occupied with his bats; she would pay more attention to him later. He kept quiet, didn't want the momentum to be lost, and guided her to the top of the toilet tank, lifted her leg, slowly pressed into her. He'd go to bed hungry, exhaustion and an apology his dinner.

■ ■ ■

He dreamed of volcanoes erupting suddenly, all at once. The town was the town he lived in but different, spread out, with houses overlooking cliffs that didn't exist. Lava poured from the angry cones, fire ash fell from above, and cracks opened in the earth. Escape wasn't likely. Standing on a strip of land, he watched the black sky descend. Heat from beneath and above consumed him.

At 4:30 a.m., startled awake from the dream, Phillip staggered to the bathroom to piss, began to dress. Work pants from the day before, a fresh T-shirt, and a collared buttonup. Back in the single room, he kneeled over Jared, woke him by smoothing his hair.

After the kid was showered and readied, he took Benita's keys from her purse and drove him, half-awake, staring out the window, to his elementary school.

"Hey, kid," he said poking him. "Before we get you to school, tell me what you're going to tell the bats when we find them."

"I love them being my friends," he mumbled. "What will you tell them?"

Phillip wasn't sure, but maybe something about how he appreciated the bats being Jared's friends. He added that he thought it'd be a good idea if Jared brought along the bats he'd been making so that his paper bats and the bats supposedly in the caves at the mountain base might become friends. The kid told him, duh, that was why he'd been cutting them out.

Benita was never awake when he returned her car in the mornings. Wouldn't stir even if he bumped the furniture or creaked the door open and closed. Girl can sleep through anything, he thought. A quality he both admired and looked down on.

He retrieved his tool bucket and drill bag, walked the two hundred yards to the bus stop. Every day the same ride across town: sparse traffic; chemical-white billows hovering above the toilet paper plant south of the train tracks; an abandoned steel mill turned junkyard that advertised auto repair and estimates; the refurbished historic downtown, beyond his price range.

At twenty past seven, he arrived at the jobsite, where Vick was waiting to tell him he was late.

"I'm this *late* every day," said Phillip. "I don't control the bus schedule. No one else arrives on time. I've got the kid to take care of, and there's no use jerking off here before seven if the gate isn't even open."

Vick waved him off, muttered, "Yeah, yeah," even though none of the other trades ever arrived before eight, and if they did it was only to stroll around with doughnuts, then fuck off for the day. Phillip was the only electrician on-site. He was reliable, his lack of a vehicle the assurance he'd stay put, and still he'd never been given a key to unlock the gate in the mornings.

While Phillip unchained and positioned the ladders, Vick brushed the rat end of his ponytail against his lips and examined the conduit runs across the ceiling, traced each run to where it ended at the service panel or hung unfinished.

"Might get close to completing the runs today," said Vick, "if you can hustle and don't fuck up. How are you on materials?"

Phillip needed spools of ground and neutral wire to begin pulling circuit boats by the end of the day, and asked if he could get off early, hoping Vick wouldn't put too much thought to it. Vick sucked the tip of his rattail, took more than a minute to respond. Wouldn't be possible. Not with all the added dedicated circuits, subpanel, phone, co-ax, and ethernet for the reception area, break room, and bathrooms. The facility was going to be top-of-the-line, filled with as many distractions as possible. The patients would want to ignore the fact that they were in a dialysis center. There would even be TVs in the pisser. All overtime for the week and, Phillip suspected, through the weekend. He reminded Vick that he'd requested time off; Vick responded that it was out his hands. But with Phillip's request in mind—which was bullshit—Vick had hired a helper. Older guy who claimed ten years' residential wiring experience and countless skills in other trades.

"Sure that's all a load of shit," said Phillip.

"That's what I'm thinking. But he's got no qualms working for ten an hour without overtime despite the experience he claims to have. Shit, if he were a Mexican, I could pay him five. Anyway, you'll probably have to teach him to bend pipe, pull wire, and whatever else. You're going to have your work cut out for you.

And I don't imagine he'll be too keen on a young tonto telling him what to do. Guy's name is Nolen or something. Told him to show up around nine. Give you time to set up and get going. I should have your materials here by then."

Vick spit a loogie on the polished concrete floor, smeared it with the toe of his boot, and walked to his truck.

After he drove away, Phillip cursed him for being an inept and ignorant piece of shit who had managed to fuck him by hiring some old lackey, probably a drunk, who would only slow Phillip's progress. Just another benign action from the managers, reminding Phillip that he was an unappreciated and unacknowledged electrician who made twelve to the ten dollars an hour his helper was going to be paid.

Around nine thirty Phillip smelled the sour stench of cigarette smoke and days-old body odor. He turned, looked down from the twelve-foot ladder at a man, probably six foot six, wearing clothes that hung off him like the tattered sails of a ghost ship, a frayed canvas duffel with black splotches slung across his back. Phillip couldn't help thinking that some carcass had bled through the bag. The man clomped across the jobsite in large desert boots, reached into what remained of a shirt pocket for a pack of cheap cigarettes, lit one using the one he'd smoked to the filter, and flicked it behind him aimlessly.

Phillip descended the ladder, uncertain if this was the guy Vick had hired or a random homeless.

"Can I help you with something?" he asked.

"That's what I'm here for," said the man. "To help you."

"All right. Vick said your name was Nolen. I'm Phillip."

The derelict man shook his head, his eyes a glacial blue.

"It's No-Lee," he said.

Phillip listened to the man's explanation: people always asked if he had any leads on any jobs and he'd tell them no, no leads. So the name No-Lee stuck. The two stared at each other until Phillip told No-Lee that he would start him on running conduit. They'd work together until No-Lee got the hang of it. It'd be easy since they were only using half-inch, a little three-quarter.

They worked atop ladders eight feet apart, the length of a single stick of conduit. At the butting end, No-Lee tightened the coupling with channel locks and secured the conduit to the base of a wooden truss with a half-inch strap, eight inches from the coupling. Phillip held the opposite end, measured off the wall to ensure a straight run, and strapped the conduit loosely. They moved across the trusswork in leapfrog fashion until they reached a point in the run that required a ninety-degree bend toward the service panel. Phillip explained the fundamentals of conduit bending: from the point of measurement mark back five inches, toward the dumb-end of the tape—six inches if using three-quarter—make sure the footpad of the conduit bender faces the foot; make sure the bend is a perfect ninety by applying equal pressure on the footpad and handle, and use a level to be precise.

No-Lee repeated the instructions, and the conduit installation continued smoothly, faster than Phillip had expected. By two in the afternoon, he estimated they'd accomplished a little more than the day's anticipated tasks. Two more days of working like this past sundown, and Saturday would be secured.

"I'm going to hit up the gas station on the corner for a quick lunch," said Phillip. "Need anything?"

No-Lee limped to where the breeze was strongest and sat, lighting up a cigarette, his eyes closed as if prepared to gather substance from the tobacco smoke and wind. He hacked to clear his throat and swallowed.

"Pack of their cheapest unfiltereds. Bottle of honey and cay-enne powder or hot sauce if they got it," he said, shoving his hand into his pants pockets and removing a bill that looked like rotten spinach.

"Don't worry about it," said Phillip. "Get me back on Friday when we'll get fresh bills."

No-Lee returned the money to his pocket, shrugged, and said, "Your loss."

Phillip returned with a microwave burrito, a dollar bag of chips, and a gallon of water for himself. He placed a bear-shaped bottle of honey, a small bottle of Tabasco, and a nondescript pack of cigarettes next to No-Lee, who appeared to be napping, then opened one eye.

"You eat that shit every day?" he asked.

"It's cheap," said Phillip. "I don't have time to make lunch. I've got the kid I take care of. Eats up most of my time."

"You got a kid?"

"Not mine. My cousin's. I raise him here so he can go to a de-cent school, have more opportunity or whatever."

"Mother drank herself to death, huh?"

Phillip crumpled his burrito wrapper, threw it, and it was suspended for a second, then was blown backward.

He was used to this passive-aggressive, often plainly aggres-sive, shit-talk from White, conservative coworkers and bosses. Back in Phoenix, the ignorance strong, and everywhere, as much as there was heat and blowing dust. Proud right-wingers who boasted about the guns kept locked in their glove boxes, some with handguns strapped to their hips, talking God and country, rights, and who deserved to live and who to die. Sad harbingers of death that Phillip could only do his best to ignore, though he was often confronted by them because he was brown, often mistaken for a Mexican, and always given a pass because he wasn't *them*, but neither was he an *us*.

"No one in my family drinks," he said. "The kid's mom fucked off to Portland with a bunch of vortex, vision-questing dykes."

No-Lee drew long, the cigarette ember flexed; dragon smoke poured from his nostrils.

"Bitch can't appreciate her own dying culture. Funny. All that pride you redskins powwow about, and most of you fall for new age bullshit. You sell out your faith, then build fucking casinos."

Phillip ate his last chip, dropped the bag, and told his helper to sit and smoke for the rest of the lunch hour while he got back to it. No-Lee responded, "I work when you work, and I was told to clean up." He stood, examined the jobsite, which was without clutter except for some unusable scraps of conduit and the trash Phillip had tossed. No-Lee picked up the burrito wrapper and chip bag, stuffed them into his pocket, and organized the material without comment. The exhalation of smoke and the gurgled hack of clearing his throat were his only noises.

Phillip called the day sometime after seven, watched No-Lee walk east beneath the streetlights until he became a burned match in the distance. He made note of the next day's work—pull boats, pull lighting circuits, low volt, land the panel—grabbed his gear, and trudged to the bus stop.

■ ■ ■

He arrived back to his place late. It sat dark, lifeless, between the noisy brightness of the rooms on either side. The curious tunnel of it drew him in. Benita had left a folded note on the table. The explanation was simple: she needed to finish out her final semester in the dorms and concentrate and had left Jared with the manager. Anger shook Phillip's throat and he punched two holes in the wall: one for being abandoned, the other for having to bear the burden of an abandoned child. He smashed one of the two chairs against the matted carpet until no right angles remained, and cursed and hit himself over the head before hurrying to clean up the splintered pieces.

On his way to the manager's office, he gathered himself by tapping his chest, imagining himself and the kid excited, standing, out of breath, before the mouth of a cave. They'd enter a cool, damp darkness, shine lights on walls that held something he couldn't think of. In the office, Jared and the manager watched a cartoon show Phillip didn't recognize, their laughter settling the tension in his shoulders. He watched for a few minutes before announcing himself. It wasn't a big thing for the manager, since Jared hadn't ever been a problem, but it also couldn't keep happening. Phillip needed to figure it out. Back in the room, he and Jared continued watching the cartoon until both dozed and slept, their shadows playing oddly on the wall behind them.

■ ■ ■

The morning bus that took Phillip and the kid to a stop a quarter-mile walk from school was empty. At the school, they waited until the doors opened for students who needed an early drop-off. The kid told Phillip that Benita would come back, that she'd cried before taking him to the manager's office. The kid was probably right, Phillip told him. They'd have a boys' weekend. Afterward everything would be the same.

At the jobsite, No-Lee sat against the locked gate smoking,

his empty, dirty duffel crumpled on his lap. It was close to eight, with no sign of Vick. Phillip made the decision to dismantle the tension bands, the chain-link fence fell slack, and the two crouched and went through. Let Vick fix the goddamned thing, they needed to get to work.

When they stopped for lunch, No-Lee asked for honey and hot sauce again.

"What do you need those two things for?" asked Phillip.

"Mix them together to create a perimeter when I bivouac or shelter in a cave. Keeps the bugs off me, especially the goddamned ants."

"So you're not staying anywhere," said Phillip.

"I just said I bivouac or shelter in caves. You're a trog. You should know about shelter and caves. Or has that been lost to you too?"

Vick arrived well after lunch and shouted at Phillip for fucking up the fence, went on about added cost and time. But the fence wasn't damaged, Phillip said, only taken apart, and if Vick actually knew anything, he could reassemble it. In response, Vick threatened to fire Phillip, who packed up his tools and walked furiously out of the gate, where he was stopped, told to calm down, and asked what was needed to fix the fencing. Phillip told Vick that No-Lee knew. So the two of them reassembled the tension bands, spoke quietly, and looked and nodded toward Phillip, who hung the wire spools and began pulling circuit boats to the junction boxes like a man possessed. Something he did alone easily, hoping that Vick took his time before fucking off again.

Before the day's light began to fade, Phillip told No-Lee he needed to leave to pick up and then return with the kid.

"You work late Fridays?" No-Lee asked.

"Twelve to fourteen is average. I don't care if we work all night. We're getting this shit done."

"Whatever you say," said No-Lee. "I've got my money. See you later."

It took an hour to get the kid. What daylight remained cast long shadows. The gate was locked. Beyond the cold links, Phillip saw that the ladders had been left standing. He told the kid to wait and jumped the fence. Inside, the material lay scattered, ransacked for any pieces of value. His tool bucket was gone, along with a couple of spools of solid ground wire. An old, stained dollar bill was attached to one of the exposed metal studs with a drywall screw. Written in black marker, almost clownishly, along the galvanized steel stud was the word *Tanks*.

Phillip's head spun. A hollowness opened in his chest, dropping him to his knees. He screamed into his shirt. No-Lee had certainly waited for a moment like this, Phillip's stressed modicum of trust, so he could leave him fucked. No regard for his livelihood, his need to care for himself and the kid. He dialed Vick, got voice mail right away. Piece of shit had already disappeared into the weekend, obviously hadn't even returned to check on the jobsite.

He stood, pixelated among the shadows, and threw his phone against the polished concrete, its shattered pieces skipping outward. He turned and jumped the fence again.

"To hell with all this," he said. "I'm fucked."

The kid pulled at Phillip's dry and hardened hand. "It's okay. It's okay. We can be okay. There's a phone in the room and the bats are there. We can be okay."

Phillip squeezed his temples with one hand, and with the other he returned the kid's grip. They walked to the corner gas station for a couple of dinner burritos and provisions for their cave trek.

■ ■ ■

Phillip stirred, woke to see Jared dressed, his pile of cutout bats ready on the table. The kid didn't mess around. He sat in the unbroken chair gazing out the window at thunderheads separated by cuts of sunlight that made dew of the predawn sprinkle. It was well past their planned departure time. The kid slid off his chair, opened the door: the crisp, cool scent of vanilla from the ponderosas and the dusty mold of the morning's moisture engulfed the room.

"Guess I better get my lazy ass in gear, huh? Let me shower and we'll get the hell out of here," he said, rubbing his puffy face.

The kid nodded, shut the door, and began to gather the bottles of water, granola bars, and two Snickers that Phillip had bought the day before. He took the flashlight from the nightstand drawer, located both his and Phillip's bus passes.

The trailhead lay northwest of them. The nearest bus stop was next to a grocery store, where Phillip lifted two oranges from an outside display of produce. He told the kid they needed to survive, and they started their trek. Beneath the shade of large ponderosas, they paused to eat the oranges. Phillip asked the kid if he was hanging in there okay, there was a mile and a half left to go. The kid said he was fine; they'd go on, they'd survive. The two pushed forward and the day warmed up, a little humid from the morning's rain. Phillip felt the hardened shell of his heel crack, the tender flesh beneath sticking to his sock, and slowed his pace. The kid noticed, told Phillip there was no need to rush, the bats would be there. They stopped once more where the tree line broke into a clear-cut for a natural gas pipeline and service road. Logs were piled into long triangles about twenty feet from the treed edge, the brush cleared for the fire crews who would complete the controlled burns. Across the road the trail ascended into tree shade.

The mountain base was a jumble of volcanic boulders and hardened lava flows where climbers might easily traverse the rock face. Lichen and an assortment of small trees, ferns, and cacti covered the unreachable parts, higher on the rocky ledges. The cover of tall ponderosa pines made the day appear later than it was. Phillip and the kid walked along the base until they came upon a faint path that led off the trail and into a cluster of ferns.

"Looks like a deer trail, maybe some other animal," said Phillip. "There are too many dead pine needles to be sure."

Beyond the green fanlike leaves, a patch of hard-packed earth and seat-sized rocks lay below a small, man-size entrance into the boulders. Phillip suggested they eat more before entering. The kid ate quickly, reached into his pocket for his pile of bats, peeled one off, and handed it to Phillip, asked him to read its body.

"It just looks like notes from the bottom of the pages," said Phillip. "This bat must be a nerd. Hand me a different one."

The kid laughed, set the bat in what he deemed the nerd pile, and peeled another off.

"Let's see, it says, '11 Again, if two lie together, then they have heat: but how can one be warm alone? 12 And if one prevail against him, two shall withstand him; and a threefold cord is not quickly broken. 13 Better is a poor and a wise child than an old and foolish king, who will no more be admonished.' Damn, kid, these Bible bats are fucking intense. Let's see one more."

The kid peeled off bat after bat while Phillip read their bodies. He admired Jared's meticulous handiwork as the small pile grew.

Some dexterity was required to enter the cave's mouth, though it wasn't a tight squeeze. Cool air caressed Phillip's face with the faint scent of honey and chili; a heavy waft of rancid urine, body odor, and alcohol followed. Water trickled in the darkness. Once inside and on flat ground, Phillip flicked on the flashlight the kid had packed and shone it toward the sound of the trickling. A wavering figure, more beast than man, pissed against the far wall.

"You gonna come suck this thing or fuck off with that light?" A voice broken by smoke and drink emanated from a grotesque swell of skin that was a face, a bloodshot rage in its eyes.

Phillip panicked, more for the kid's safety than his own, and hurried to push Jared back before he fully entered, but the kid tumbled off the rocks and onto the cave floor. He yelped painfully, and lay holding his ankle in the faint light of the entrance. Phillip knelt to urge the kid up, didn't see the spool of neutral wire come flying through the darkness. The hard weight struck his temple and he swirled into the void of his volcano dreams: pools and rivers of lava, the burning of his face and body, the burning of Jared's and Benita's bodies, screaming and laughter from someplace far.

"I was hoping you were some bitch," echoed the voice. "Ain't easy for a guy like me to get any gash out here."

Phillip stood unsteadily, felt blood beating out of his head, and fell back on his ass. He'd fucked up, he knew, in the whirlwind of the week's events. He recognized the grated voice, the degenerate man who owned it.

He couldn't see No-Lee or the kid, but he heard Jared's frightened sobs, the twist of a plastic cap against glass. He listened as

No-Lee swallowed hard twice, twisted the cap back on. Heard the whoosh of something tumbling through the musty cave air and shattering near the kid's whimpering. No-Lee laughed, gagged from the effort. Phillip rose and rushed into the black toward the sound; arms bent to ninety at the elbow, hands curled to grasp what he could of No-Lee. When his hands met the man's chest, he gripped and drove his shirt collar into his neck. The two grappled, staggered in the darkness, until No-Lee began to vomit and threw his body into Phillip's, and they fell hard against the wall and ground. An object was knocked over and others crashed out of it. From what Phillip could feel with his hands and body, No-Lee was on his side, back against Phillip's knees. He skimmed his right hand across the dirt, found what felt like a screwdriver. His left hand found the hair on the back of No-Lee's head, gripped it tight. He rolled himself over until he felt he was on top of No-Lee's back. He brought the screwdriver down onto No-Lee's head quickly, with force. The body beneath him bucked. Phillip struck his own left hand deeply on his second stabbing attempt, and his grip on No-Lee's hair went slack. So he hugged No-Lee's head, shook it like he had Jared's head when he was a small child and would ask to be picked up by Phillip, to be swung back and forth so his legs looked like a pendulum. No-Lee's neck cracked; his body went limp. Phillip collapsed, took his gashed hand in his shirt, and tried to focus on the dimming light at the cave entrance.

∎ ∎ ∎

Phillip had never carried a gun before working in Phoenix. He'd only plinked cans off dirt mounds with small-caliber rifles out on the rez with his cousins. The day he decided to carry, a short

Guatemalan man was hired to remove the stucco and chicken wire siding for an addition. Racial slurs and death threats were being slung at the man because he hadn't completed the task before Phillip and his boss showed up to remove the electrical wiring and outlets so the framing could be redone. He remembered the man's fearful expression and watery eyes, the erratic swing of his sledgehammer and his pleas in Spanish. The other contractors stood by in a semicircle, showed one another their pistols and crossed the man with the short barrel ends. Carrying a piece would be a temporary thing for Phillip. He decided to sell the handgun to a cousin for a couple hundred less than what he had paid for it after he became the target, the contractors and other tradesmen directing their attacks at him. He was viewed as no different from the hated Central and South American migrant workers, his skin as brown as theirs. Outgunned, with no recourse to the Phoenix police, because they would certainly shoot him down, Phillip felt his anger and humiliation fester. He judged, began to hate anyone paler than he was. He often dreamed of shooting the racists, the far-right-wingers, torching whatever ignorant, upper-class project they were working on, and letting everyone and everything burn to ash.

The kid wasn't crying anymore when he shook Phillip awake, shone the flashlight in his eyes.

"Are you cool? Are you cool?" he repeated, until Phillip told him he was.

"I want to go home," he said. "We need to go home."

Phillip sat up and held the kid, told him, "Okay."

Outside, a breeze rustled the pine needles, and a faraway dog barked once. Phillip felt nauseated and weak, the sensation of the air on his skin made him aware of the heat flaring within him. He was lost, without purpose, and wanted a solution, needed one to be given to him. He thought of the body in the cave, his tools. He told the kid to wait and gathered his livelihood scattered around the cave, leaving the tainted screwdriver plunged into No-Lee's cheek. Outside, he smoothed Jared's hair, told him to keep watch over the tool bucket and drill bag with his bats. The kid nodded, took the bats from his pocket, and held them. Phillip headed toward the pipeline road, some sixty feet through the ponderosas, to a burn pile. Something needed to be done about No-Lee's hateful body, it'd be found sooner or later. Phillip estimated half an hour to forty-five minutes, if he hustled and didn't fuck up, in order to remove enough logs to cover No-Lee's body back in the cave before the forest gave way to complete darkness. He would burn the motherfucker. Char any evidence of his or the kid's ever being there. After, he and the kid would walk beneath the night, find a pay phone, if pay phones still existed, and call Benita, beg a ride back to the motel. She'd give in; she would, for him or the kid, it didn't matter.

When Phillip had finished building a pyre of logs over the reeking body, he stuffed the gaps with dried pine needles and twigs. Jared climbed into the cave quietly and sat next to where Phillip knelt, peeled off one of his Bible bats, and placed it in a space between the logs.

"We'll leave them. The bats will protect us," said the kid.

Phillip hiccupped and fought back tears. He smoothed Jared's coarse hair and helped place the bats in cracks along the perimeter of the stacked logs. He ignited the kindling on the far side of the pyre while the kid watched. It took flame, illuminating the already-blackened walls of the cave, and the two noticed how the smoke wafted up through a natural chimney in the rock. As the paper bats burned, their curled bodies drifted upward until the ash and char of them filled the interior. When the whole pyre began to burn and the smoke was too much, they left, retrieved Phillip's tools. On the far side of the service road, they turned around, saw nothing of fire or smoke in the darkness.

Phillip's tongue fat and coarse in his mouth, he asked the kid if he was thirsty. He was. But both were without water.

As Meaningless as the Origin

After the continuous days of drying gypsum and cleaning the hawk and trowel with cold bucket-water, my hands had stiffened, the skin between my fingers split.

The homeowner, a fat-handed computer tech from the Northwest, watched as Lucas and I washed drywall mud off our heads and bodies. He kept thanking us for all our hard work. It took artisans like us to float out such smooth, no-texture walls. We doubted his automatic, meaningless sincerities. Despite having met the bid, we'd gone a week over the estimated month and had never addressed the homeowner with anything but degradation. We knew no one else would have driven out this far to hang Sheetrock for a guy who had made many attempts to top the workday off with Earl Grey and female pop music.

Lucas had said, "Listen, this isn't a fucking bathhouse, asshole. Why don't you go ogle some *twinky* internet fucks instead?"

I wouldn't have called the homeowner a pushover. He certainly had the slumped demeanor of someone used to antagonism.

But he was thick-skinned enough to respond confidently because of the financial gain he'd made in his life.

"I wasn't *ogling*," he said. "I just thought that you two looked like skinheads. Anyway, your payment is under a rock on the front porch."

He slammed his back door, frowning. The translucent figures of Lucas and me were mirrored on the glass, and beyond them, he stared doubtfully at his wet gypsum walls. They'd take two days to dry until he could paint over them, which we hadn't told him.

"Sassy bitch," said Lucas.

"Fucking right," I said. "What skinheads do you know who're Navajo? Should have told him that the noble days of braids and mullets are over, and motherfuckers who don't want to pay forty on a haircut keep it close."

Lucas said, "He'll rot along with his house. There isn't anybody who'll do the upkeep. This place will be an abandoned shell. Let's get out of here."

We dried ourselves with our shirts, gathered our tools, and loaded them into my truck. I finished off a joint while Lucas went to grab the money. I watched as he bent down and picked up what looked like two checks instead of the cash we'd agreed on. Lucas shoved both rectangular pieces of paper into his pants pocket, undid his fly, and pissed on the front porch. The nasal squeak of some pubescent singer blared from the rear of the house while I turned to stare at the faint eastern horizon, then back to the throbbing shell. There was no evidence that Lucas or I had ever been there. Nothing of our thoughts to be considered. Nothing in the structure or trim that held any personality. Our work was as meaningless as the origin of any of the material used in constructing the place.

We laughed at its plain simplicity and left.

■ ■ ■

Now, as the sky swallows the silhouette of Humphrey's Peak, the highway becomes a darkened corridor of trees. The dual center-lines of the road stream yellow through the curves and hills, the distance ahead discernible in the weak beam of the truck's headlights.

Lucas tells me he intends to make New Orleans a week after I make Alaska, my flight in a few days. The bus ticket south is cheap, and they don't hassle anyone for IDs; the long, cramped trip is worth the inevitable claustrophobia. He imagines that by pursuing the woman he's infatuated with, Denise, to another city, love is inevitable. They can start a life together in some in-expensive shithole—it'll all work out in a different locale, new and unknown possibilities. My old high school buddy's mother moved to Alaska and has a boyfriend in need of framers—idiots who can sink nails, do basic addition, work twelve-hour days, and live on an island. The toughest part about the job, my buddy said, was the seclusion, the limits of escape. I won't know what I'm in for until I can judge what surrounds me, decide what's meant by limits.

Once we get to town, Lucas and I plan one final trip to Cherry Pie's Gentlemen's Club, a small and destitute strip joint in the clogged heart of Flagstaff. It was built as an addition to the back storage room of a dank bar frequented by midafternoon drunks and tradesmen looking for cheap swill and the unattainable col-lege girls who pregame there before heading to the packed meat market bars. Lucas and I had hung and taped the Sheetrock, painted the walls matte black, and installed all the mirrors over the course of a few days some months back. The owner shorted us on the final bill, always vanishing whenever we showed up, and so we started drinking there. The bartenders rarely tabbed us out at over twenty bucks apiece, no matter how many we threw back or how long we stayed. So not being paid in cash and having to deal with the checks later won't keep us from the inebriated normality of our final night out.

We don't look forward to running into anyone, the relationships we've both had as short-lived as memories after late evenings. We talk about no longer having to listen to, or hear about, the impossible projects of self-glorified handymen who never have the right tools, timeline, or helpers to fund their functional alcoholism; housepainters who claim secret lives as artists and who hijack the traditional iconography and style of more successful Native painters and blame their lack of success on affirmative action; live-in tourists who own second homes and who bitch that the town needs more gentrification, the poverty-with-a-view sentiment no longer authentic; the unspoken club of good-ol'-boys who hire and contract among themselves so that most builders are the same hungover potheads who construct every other piece-of-shit subdivision. We commiserate further until we recognize that neither of us has an address that we're destined to—we've made no living arrangements—and that email will have to replace handwritten letters, which we'll lose interest in writing once the repetitive nature of our days sets in. The only thing, we agree, that'll keep us connected will be a similar list of past letdowns and annoyances, which we'll summon up alone in a bar, when we've related to nothing in our new settings, and we will reminisce about what better days were had. That is, until those memories begin fading and we become nothing to no one.

"It's like the job we just finished," says Lucas. "You're in it until it's done. Then you're on to the next one. The only thing you take is what you've learned from unforeseen problems and ways around them. Troubleshoot—you learn how to troubleshoot and improvise."

Lucas is the most asked-for laborer in town. Whether it's for tear-outs, trench work, drywall, carpentry, or tile, he's the first on many contractors' lists. His back and body outlast most, and he hardly bitches. He's been told that his mind's stronger than his body, the combination of the two giving him the potential to work anywhere—though I've known him to numb his thoughts repeatedly, and I have witnessed the strain of his exhaustion and restlessness.

"What I'll really remember is the sunset across the desert," he says. "Nothing particular or detailed. Just the light across the landscape and then it being taken away by shadows."

The first time I met Lucas, he body-checked me into a wall during a mosh pit at a metal show that featured local bands along with a few other bands from the rez. It was one of those early-evening-to-last-call events, the crowd getting more raucous and rowdier as the music thrashed on. My shoulder had put a large hole in the drywall, and before the bartender threatened to kick us out, we both assured him that we had the skills to re-pair the damage, along with any other blemishes that needed attention. We arrived the following morning, hungover. In ad-dition to our taste in music, we found commonality in using the blowout-patch as the most efficient repair method. By cut-ting the Sheetrock an inch larger around the perimeter of the hole, then scoring and peeling back the excess so that a flap of the paper remained, the taping could be skipped, and the float-ing out done smoother, quicker.

∎ ∎ ∎

We pull up to a red light at the Highway 89 and Townsend-Winona intersection. The northbound traffic is heavy toward Cameron, Gray Mountain, and Tuba City, with families who have come to town from the Navajo Nation, and who are returning now, after having spent a few hours at the mall, downtown, or at the theater, taking in a couple of flicks.

Lucas exits the cab and hefts himself quickly into the truck bed. He taps the rear sliding window, leans against the toolbox, lighting a cigarette. I release the window lock and Lucas slides it open, his facial features choleric from the glow of the sodium-vapor streetlights.

"Turn the music up," he says.

After increasing the volume, I roll my window down a bit so the smoke doesn't hover and blow through the cab. The sounds of the wind and music make for no conversation.

Driving into Flagstaff with the moonless sky above, I look for Navajo transients along the sidewalks stumbling drunk. At this hour of evening, some are bound to be gathering, combining whatever drinks they've been able to bum, and disappearing into the woods. Anglo locals see the drunks as destitute pests, always hustling with the same story of how they just need a few more bucks for a bus ticket out. The way these locals tell it, it seems as if every Navajo, every Native person, is like this, as if our entire population exists on handouts and escapism—they dismiss a culture's minute percentage of fuckups as an epidemic.

I consider the lights cutting the darkness—cars, convenience stores, local-business signs advertising tin sheds and fencing—the depth of their illumination shallow compared with this land's expanse and terrain. I think of the move to Alaska during the beginning of summer, the possibility of the sun never setting. The guy needing framers warned me that the sun doesn't really go down. Instead, the sky is like twilight or dusk for a few hours. There isn't a complete transition. And once you've adjusted to summer's evenings, the coming winter pisses rain under darkness, and the sensation of twilight or dusk begins again, only to signify day rather than night.

This seems irrational, like a hallucinatory setting for insomniacs.

■ ■ ■

The last time we were at Cherry Pie's, Lucas got blackout drunk— I wavered on its murky edges—and passed out during a lap dance from a girl whose stage name was either Destiny or Dawn, and whom he had slept with back when the place first opened. She was rightly pissed, emotionally bruised, her ego gut-punched. I think she might have had a thing for Lucas beyond the sultry demeanor she put on for work. After that we drank at the bar only in the early evenings on weekdays. Lucas denied being embarrassed, and I reminded him that it was I who had to bear the weight of knowing a guy who was bored by lap dances.

Lucas and I order a round of beers and whiskey shots. We shoot the liquor, tap the bar with our glasses for another round, and scan the place. Both pool tables are taken, and the second-hand couch near the fireplace is occupied by two polo shirt–wearing bro-dudes and a girl dressed in a shiny, skimpy answer.

"Think they're all just friends?" asks Lucas.

"Sure," I say, "until they start fucking each other and one of those two assholes gets possessive."

We laugh and clink cans, throw back our burns of whiskey.

"I'm not going to miss any of this shit," says Lucas.

"No, you won't. You'll feel the rush of someplace new. You can be less than no one. And by the time you get bored or broken-hearted, it'll all begin to seem like the same old shit again."

Lucas shakes his head. Denise has been locked up for hooking herself a way out of town and in care facilities for breakdowns, suicide attempts—either way, there's a lot of passion. Her past boyfriends have usually been drug dealers, keeping her dosed, calm. With Lucas it's the threat of his temper, the comfort of his physical strength over hers. I haven't been with a woman for more than a few nights, with months and months between those lucky moments, and I haven't kept an apartment for more than half a year. A modern-day nomad, though, to be honest, I don't know what I'm working toward and haven't stayed still long enough for loneliness to take root and blossom.

"Listen," he says. "You want my advice. I've traveled with only a bag on my back and had to begin where I didn't intend to be. Don't do more than you think you can handle. You'll only fuck yourself. That's it. Don't do more than you can handle."

Lucas has always alluded to growing up in affluence. Ivy League assurance, high-rise condos, parents something to do with dignitaries between Ontario and Poland. He had hit the road in a van with guys bound for California. The transmission blew in Arizona, sixty miles east of Flagstaff. Lucas was the only one who stayed, having found a junk-collecting woman who allowed him to pitch a tent on her lot next to a wall of broken refrigerators.

"I'm learning what I can handle as I go along," I say. "But I expect that I'll take on too much at some point. It's the only way to really know your limits."

Lucas nods, drinks his beer.

We watch the two polo shirts leave, with the skimpy dress

following. She turns and smiles in our direction but not at us; her happiness isn't for us; neither is it for the boys she trails. Lucas and I avert our glances as she vanishes through the door.

An hour passes, maybe two.

A guy who's laid tile on some of the jobs we've worked shoves his head between Lucas and me. We'd both been staring into our beers and shots quietly; I was thinking about seclusion and anonymity giving me the space to become someone new. Lucas was thinking about his girl, probably.

"That better be whiskey," says Conroy. Lucas and I both shrug.

Conroy's voice sounds like he's holding vomit back or has been recently choked. He takes pride in smoking a pack of un-filtereds daily, eating bacon sandwiches, owning body armor hammer-molded out of aluminum sheets. He claims to have neo-Nazi associations—we suspect his so-called *association* is a self-conscious fantasy that justifies his balding head. There's nothing in Conroy's features that suggests any trace of Aryan blood.

"It's good to see two rough, hardworking sons of bitches out tonight. I just rolled up my job. Mind if I sit?" Conroy takes a stool on the other side of Lucas, placing his forearms, splotched with grout that appears leprous over his tattoos, on top of the bar. We'd first encountered Conroy while patching holes made by electricians; he reminded us continually not to get drywall mud in his grout lines. He took to Lucas and me because we'd play black metal on the stereo, and from that he assumed we were like him. We weren't. He was just one more lowbrow trades-man eager to drink.

"Sit where you want," says Lucas, "just get the next round."

"Not a problem," says Conroy waving down the bartender. "Three of whatever firewaters these two have been drinking."

Raising his shot, Conroy makes a toast to the American working class and national brotherhood. He calls Lucas "brother" and me "chief." Neither Lucas nor I drink. Instead, we place our shots down on the bar. Lucas knows I'm never cool with a stranger's or an acquaintance's stereotyped jests, especially if ignorant or unintentional. As for Lucas, he's easily annoyed with dismissive idiots mucking around in bastardized entitlement.

Lucas pushes the shots toward Conroy and tells him, "You need to dull your stupidity and catch up."

"Come on," says Conroy. "I know it's been a long day for you too. What you two refusing for?"

"Just catch up," says Lucas, making an opened-handed gesture.

Conroy insists again, agitated and taking offense.

Lucas tells him, "Listen, don't be a pussy. If you're all you think you are, you won't let a Polack and Trog drink you under the bar. What would be the pride in that? Now catch up."

Conroy looks frustrated and confused. He says, "I never made you for a Polack, man. You're not a Jew, are you?"

Lucas answers, "No."

Conroy shoots one shot. He looks at me and I think of how satisfying it'd be to just glass him, except I'm drinking from a can. Lucas knows what I'm thinking, because, as Conroy is focused on me, Lucas holds his beer and mocks slamming it against Conroy's head.

"He's right," I say. "You can't just let us drink you under the bar."

Conroy smiles, takes the remaining shot.

Lucas orders more rounds.

The conversation shifts to metal genres and mosh-pitting, the three of us differentiating the nuances of satanic, black, thrash, satanic-black, gore, gore-thrash, sludge, grind, dirty-black, and experimental. Conroy's inability to understand anything beyond satanic-black metal bands, generally from Nordic regions, leads him to tell us that his girlfriend is stripping tonight, and that we should watch her because she'll strip to anything metal, and he wants to hear some metal.

Lucas leans close to me, says, "Shit, man, I think I want to see what lame bitch would allow this loser's prick inside her."

I agree that I'm curious about the sexual preferences of racists—the physical features—and wonder if their spawn will turn out just as ugly and inarticulate. Lucas agrees, since Conroy will be picking up the rounds.

Avoiding the seats around the stage, the three of us post up at the bar in the corner, where we won't be expected to tip the girls who are performing. We won't be approached for private dances, since Lucas fell asleep and I'm his known associate.

Conroy orders a round and this time he doesn't say shit about anything as he takes his shot. Instead, he walks over to a thick-thighed, tiny-titted girl with black hair cut in the fashion of a skin-chick, long, sharp bangs with the rest buzzed short. She's flirting with a customer, a Native-looking guy—Pima, maybe—who acts as if he's used to the attention of half-naked White women trying to get money off him. It's a job, I think: you're in it for the wages no matter your dislike of the client. Conroy stands before them, his back to me so I can't see his expression. The Pima has his hands up, obviously annoyed, his mouth moving quickly. Conroy turns his head toward the guy a few times before gulping his drink and pointing at him while talking. The girl intervenes, standing now with a hand on Conroy's chest. The Pima nods, smiling at the girl's ass, which isn't bad, and Conroy takes the girl's hand and attempts to move it. A bouncer and the bartender run and grab Conroy, pulling him back toward Lucas and me, while the girl makes apologetic gestures to the Pima as she leads him toward the walled-off private dance area.

Conroy's face is red, spittle on his chin. He looks at the ground as the bartender tells him to keep cool and assures the bouncer, who's new, that everything's a misunderstanding. Conroy picked the wrong time to talk with his girl. The bouncer returns to his spot in the shadows, and the bartender, patting Conroy's back, walks behind the bar and pours us one on the house.

"Damn," says Lucas. "I'm getting slightly shitty."

"Same here," I say, looking into my glass and swirling the liquid.

Conroy leans over to me, saying, "What the fuck's the problem with your shit-stain cousin over there? He can't see that I'm trying to talk to my woman. That redskin thinks he has some sort of right being here. Shit."

"It's a strip joint," I say. "You interrupted a business transaction. Besides, I'm Navajo, asshole. I don't have shit to do with Pimas. We've got different beliefs and everything. I can't speak for him."

Conroy makes the noise of a punctured tire with his mouth. "Fuck it. I need a joint. Let's go to my place. I've got whiskey there too."

While Conroy makes his way out of the club, Lucas and I stare at each other, looking for an expression of agreement. Lucas smiles.

"What's the deal with this prick? He's so dejected that he has to invite us over after saying stupid shit to both of us, then tries showing off his lump of a girlfriend? But, hell, free whiskey is free whiskey."

"True. I'm down for a joint. But I thought skinheads only smoked meth. I'm pretty sick of his bullshit, though."

"Forget about it," says Lucas. "We'll handle it, everything will be all right."

Walking outside it seems as if the night's brighter than the strip joint's interior. I look back, thinking that only the matte black walls, the mirrors, lights, pole, faux-velvet-and-vinyl-seats will remain the same, the atmospheric voice of the DJ a steady and placating drone. The rest is interchangeable: the bouncers, the girls, the customers. And it seems we're all the same person coming from work with money meant for better things; coming from a job we lost, wishing that the next one lasts long enough to get us by; coming from nowhere only to follow someone who needs something from us into a room where we hope they at least turn on the light before closing us in.

■ ■ ■

On the wall above a small television, there's a cracked mirror advertising Danish beer. The coffee table is piled with titty and skin-art magazines and an overflowing ashtray. On the floor, cigarette butts from previous nights. Empties and pizza boxes decorate the kitchen counters, complemented by the empties and pizza boxes in the dining area. Laundry hangs out of a doorway, snot-like.

"Looks like my place," I say to Lucas, "if I wasn't so clean and couldn't read."

"I wouldn't have expected less," says Lucas.

Sitting on the couch, Lucas purposefully overturns the ashtray onto the coffee table, and though it gives me a sense of uncertainty, I see that it makes no difference to the mess already there.

"What? You come over here to trash my house?" Conroy asks, bringing out plastic cups and a bottle of whiskey.

"There's no adding to this heap," says Lucas. "Can't you get that girl of yours to clean all this up?"

Conroy hands us empty cups, pours himself a belt, and sets the bottle down. He drinks, holding the burn in his mouth and, looking at us, swallows hard.

"She'll do whatever I say," he says. "I just don't need you Polacks and Trogs fucking up my house any more than I want it to be. Remember, this is my house."

Conroy finishes whatever's left in his cup and staggers to the rear of the house, toward what's probably a bedroom.

"What the fuck?" I ask Lucas. "I mean, the guy's a dipshit and we're drunk and all, but why do you want to get him worked up?"

"Because fuck him," says Lucas. "He won't do shit. He'll come back, we'll have some shots, and we'll get out of here, probably laughing our asses off. We'll handle it."

From the slack smile on Lucas's face, I can tell he's drunk, drunk as any of us. He's pale, and he picks the bottle up, drinking straight from it.

I set my cup down and lean back on the couch, mimicking patience, a calm assertion that all we have to do is leave. In Alaska, I'll live in Sitka, the only town on Baranof Island. It stretches along the western coast for about fifteen miles and extends inland only about two or three. The entire island's nearly a hundred miles long and about twenty wide, with mountains jutting skyward, and is so densely forested that to lay a foundation one has to dig through dirt and thousands of roots just to hit solid rock. It could be two feet, it could be twenty-five, it could never happen. The town's a Russian Orthodox settlement and home to Tlingit and Haida tribes. It doesn't seem so far from this room. It's beyond the door—it's a flight.

When Conroy approaches quietly from behind the couch, it's as if his sight has left him. He is guided only by the inten-

tion of the tiny gun in his hand. A .22 millimeter of some sort—
the kind priced inexpensively, intended for women's purses.
There's a cheap plastic swastika glued to the butt-end of the gun.
Conroy hasn't cocked the hammer and his finger is cinched
tightly around the trigger.

Lucas stares at the gun, takes two gulps from the bottle. The
dark circles around his eyes seem permanent, like the black
blood of his head is bleeding through.

"That's a cute little thing," says Lucas. "Where'd you get it
from?"

Conroy appears patient, entranced.

"It's my woman's," he says. "She's supposed to keep it with her."

"Well, what you doing with it?" replies Lucas. "You just showing it off?"

Conroy doesn't reply—he's as lost for words as I am. He begins taking deep, quick breaths and turns red. I turn to Lucas to
tell him we should apologize and go but think it's Conroy I need
to speak to, tell him to chill and to break out the joint. Instead, I
say nothing, doubting that I'd remain cool and confident if the
gun were pointed at me.

"My father's father came to this" is all Conroy's able to get out as
Lucas rises from the couch and hits him once, the bottle not shattering, and then a second time on the opposite side of his head.

Conroy crumples down and forward. He lies on the floor as
if passed out on his way to the couch. Blood seeps from his nose,
and I don't know enough about injuries to determine if it's important or not. Lucas pours whiskey on Conroy's head, drops
the bottle next to him. We say nothing, the silence broken by
voices beyond the door that fade toward whatever late-night
destination holds the promise of more release.

I want to know that I know what Lucas was thinking, what
Conroy was thinking, what this means in terms of my departure,

what this means for my friendship with Lucas. I want to know what he'll say next, but I don't.

"Whose father didn't come here on a fucking boat," he says through his teeth. And then, smiling, "That was unforeseen. Thought he was just pouting."

I remember reading that when Alaska was purchased by the US, some of the Russians cried as their flag was replaced by the Stars and Stripes—the disintegration of their life and language like the descent into winter's darkness. And for the Tlingit and Haida, it was just another tongue of light skin occupying their homeland.

I move closer to the gun and bend down to look at it.

"There isn't even a magazine in it," I tell Lucas. "And the way he was squeezing the trigger, I doubt anything was in the chamber. What should we do with it?"

Lucas rubs his hands over his face and shakes his head like a dog. He grumbles something and then says, "Fuck. Kick it under the couch for all I care."

I do as he suggests and we both look at Conroy. Taking notice of his slight breathing, we laugh, Lucas because I think he's lost it, and me because I'm relieved.

This is a new beginning—another evening ending with the want of more of what will obscure reality—an instance of guilt flickering and instilling wishes that I was never here.

Lucas turns toward me, grabs my shoulder, and says, "We should go. We should go someplace else."

■ ■ ■

Come sunrise, last night's revelry aching in my head and behind my eyes, I see Lucas curled in the kitchenette, his coat folded on top of his boots as a makeshift pillow. Neither of us had showered properly since going straight to Cherry Pie's the night before, then leaving Conroy's racist ass brained on his living room floor. The room smells sour and rotten and, strangely, of pepper. There's a small amount of shampoo and soap left in the shower, a hand towel that's not been packed or given away, like the rest of my stuff. I'll be checking what fits into a large duffel bag, along with my framing belt and essential hand tools.

Once I'm cleansed, I dig out the crumpled checks from Lucas's pants pocket. He grumbles something inaudible, rolls onto his back, and opens one eye.

"Fucking pansy," he says, though I'm not sure if he's referring to me, Conroy, or the client who gave us the checks.

"I'll be back as soon as I can," I say. "I'm out of this place tomorrow. Shower if you want, but don't fuck anything up."

Lucas grumbles, rolls back onto his side.

On the way out of town, I grab a large black coffee at the new drive-through, which opens at 5:00 a.m. every day, the baristas always uninvitingly vibrant and chatty. Nothing is different this morning. The streets are empty, the storefronts darkened, and the grocery store parking lots desolate. I keep the speedometer at three under until I exit the city limits, then barrel at twenty over until I reach the turnoff to the computer tech's house. It's all hard-packed dirt and washboard roads until I get there.

There are lights on in the kitchen and a thread of smoke rises from the back of the house. I don't recall there being a chimney and hope I haven't arrived to a house fire that I'll have to help extinguish. I pound on the front door first, no one answers. Walking around to the back of the place, I see the computer tech wrapped in a Pendleton blanket that could, or could not be, a Navajo design. He's wearing fur-lined moccasins and sipping a large mug next to a fire he's built inside a circle of stacked imperial-red granite stones, most likely shipped from a foreign quarry. I think that all these transplant douchebags can't stop themselves from appropriating what they believe is Southwest culture for their inane home decor.

"Well," says the computer tech, "I didn't think you'd come this early. Checks not work for you?" He smirks, his little pink lips like exposed dog penises.

"Listen, man. We agreed on cash. Personally, I don't have issues cashing checks. Lucas, on the other hand—it's a real pain in the ass for him."

"Hmm. Why is that, I wonder?" says the computer tech, sipping from his mug and snuggling deeper into the blanket.

"If you have to know, dude doesn't have a state ID or driver's license. Just his Canadian passport and a visa that's expired. No bank account. Cash works best, like we agreed. But if it comes down to you needing to write a check, make it out in the full amount to me. We're both moving on in a couple days."

The computer tech wriggles his ham hands around the mug before setting it down. He sighs. "I'm not one to screw anyone over or go back on an agreement. I'm principled, as I'm certain you and your friend can comprehend."

I nod, thinking I could simply punch this guy, put his blanket in the fire. I'm here for the money, I remind myself, and not further violence.

"Now," says the computer tech, "like I expressed yesterday. Your talents are great and not undeserving of compensation. And since you've traveled all the way out here, I want to show you the one, minor issue that I have with your and your friend's handiwork. After you follow me inside and give me your assessment, you can have your cash."

"That's fine with me," I say. "We stand by our work."

Inside, the walls are drying nicely, a little faster than expected, though I don't see any cracks appearing. They look whiter and more luminescent as the sun ascends the horizon and fills the shell with its shine. The computer tech leads me through the back dining room and kitchen toward what will be his home office, empty until the arrival of his belongings. He points to the closet door header, which has been left unfinished, the drywall compound cracked and wrinkled.

"Shit, man," I say. "Don't know how we missed that. I'll get a hawk and trowel. Still have the leftover mud somewhere?"

"Kitchen pantry. And call me Berry, like the berry."

"Right. Berry. This won't take more than fifteen minutes or so."

After applying and smoothing out the small section of header with a quick-drying compound, I wait to see if the header requires any sanding. It doesn't, but I give it a few swipes with fine-grit sandpaper anyway. While I clean the hawk and trowel, Berry offers to top off my coffee for the drive back, and I accept.

Before handing me the envelope of cash, he says, "While I have you here, would you mind straightening the screw heads on the light switches and outlets? The electrician didn't seem to understand that all the screw slots should be uniform, level, and horizontal. Do you know what 'horizontal' means?"

There's no doubt in my mind that this guy's nose would burst like a carton of berries thrown off a roof. But I think he knows I wouldn't be one to strike him when my patience is tested.

"Listen. Get me a standard screwdriver, then give me the money, and let me get the hell out of here."

The homeowner smiles. "Why would *I* own anything like that?"

Instead of walking to my trunk for a screwdriver, I ask the homeowner for a butter knife, and in less than ten minutes, I make every goddamn screw slot in the house horizontal. I hand the homeowner his butter knife, and he peers at the tip like it's been permanently ruined. He hands over the envelope of cash, which I count. It's a hundred short. If Lucas were here, I think, we'd be gone already with the money. But I'm stuck, knowing I'll take the hundred-dollar hit for the unfinished header. So I take my full coffee cup and throw it against the large and immaculately white living room wall, where it explodes. The homeowner screams, "My god," and rushes to clean up the mess with his robe. I hurry out the back door and grab the Pendleton with the seemingly Navajo design and look briefly at the fire. It would be a waste, I think, and roll it up as I rush to my truck.

Placing the blanket on the passenger seat, I'm filled with euphoria. My time to flee to an imaginary home has come.

A New Place to Hide

*There is only one way to happiness and that is to cease worrying about
things which are beyond the power of our will.*   —Epictetus

When I began driving illegally, as a sort of amateur chauffeur,
I was thirteen, and this dangerous time in my life robbed me
of my innocence. No—I was gutted, my innocence excised.
My viscera were scattered across shimmering black pavement,
which was my only reliable guide through life. I was a solitary
but not lonely child, a condition I hadn't arrived at on my own.
Colonial violence. Borderland divide-and-conquer sentimen-
talisms. Assimilative educational hierarchies of race and class,
exile and abandonment. All of it natured in me. Put plainly:
I'd spent my infancy and adolescence on Dinétah, the home-
lands of The People—*my* people, I suppose. Eventually, my ide-
alistic and easily bored parents moved us to Flagstaff, an idyllic

mountain town filled with the throat-clenching nostalgia of cow-
boys and pioneering violence. Most people being cowards, that
violence was rarely enacted individually, but in a herd, dull-
mouthed bleating can easily turn into a battle chant, the stomp-
ing of small hooves a weapon of mass destruction. The town felt
like the edge of the world, and was, in fact, the western reach of
a holy land facing a glacially paced apocalypse.

■ ■ ■

Uprooted midway through the fourth grade, I was thrust into
a classroom of mostly White students, we non-Whites being a
Black boy, two Mexican girls, a half-Mexican, half-Japanese boy,
and me. We were suspicious of one another, ignorant of the
factors, beyond our control, that had brought us to such a setting, and all too willing to accept the token*ships* of our respec-
tive White schoolmate cliques. The Black boy, always chosen
first for any sort of sport, basketball in particular, was called
Muggsy Bogues, as if anyone remembered the shortest player
in NBA history; the two Mexican girls, both first-named V, were
dubbed diseased whores by the cavalier White boys who cor-
nered them into kissing and exploratory touching; and no one
knew what to make of the Mexican-Japanese boy, whom everyone called Taco Sushi, so he was ignored, which turned him into
a pariah and bully who focused his attacks on each of us, more
than once. I don't imagine he made it very far in life or has
entered law enforcement, maybe taken a menial position in poli-
tics. As for me, I was the wild Indian, the red-skinned savage,
the other, the enemy, the target for rocks and gang-ups where I
was tied to a tree and burned with imaginary fire amid cupped-
hand whooping, hands shaped into guns, barrel fingers pointed

silently at the sky. This was the town: a simulacrum of childish imagination and a lie good enough to be mistaken for destiny. At the helm of this fourth-grade massacre was Ms. Reinholdt, an older woman with skin like porcelain, who I suspected was a runaway nun. Her long, pleated plaid skirts and dark, billowy blouses cinched at the neck reminded me of the teachers back on the rez, who were all nuns. She stalked across the front of the classroom, between our rows of desks, with her chin held high, eyes darting from student to student. Her gray hair, tied tightly into a bun, had the sheen of gunmetal. She maintained a droll tone of authority, sharpened with quick "Sit"s or "Quiet"s, though not one of us was ever punished or made to feel inferior. Instead, we were assigned books to read, along with short written responses for infractions committed against the school policies, as interpreted by Ms. Reinholdt. Such infractions might include Whispering, which burned God's ears, or Dawdling, which gave Satan the opportunity for influence, so we must move, sit, or stand with purpose, with intention. For the infraction of Melancholy, which amounted to a disregard for imagination, having rebelled against participating in small-group activities for a week, I was assigned *Chitty Chitty Bang Bang*. The book was hardbound in a faded slate cloth cover, the gold lettering pressed into the spine still iridescent. I wrote about the car's large engine and horsepower, how its four-seat touring design made it comfortable enough to potentially sleep in, and how its ability to transform into a hovercraft or airplane made it the ideal getaway car, which afforded me the imagination to envision a world beyond the one I lived in: places in the book like England or France, place-names without any shape or detail in my young, naive perception. She collected my work and read it standing there next to my desk, ignoring, for once, the replied my father, a long time coming, if you ask me. He gazed at the road ahead, perhaps seeing endless possibilities, being a reluctant and ineffectual parent, a philanderer who would take up with another woman. A singer of country songs in the bars and nightclubs of Albuquerque. He dressed like a clothing-catalog cowboy, ready to ride into the sunset on the back of almost any creature he came across. Clifton Francisco, bastard son of a Spaniard priest, his mother of the Ta'neezsani Clan, which means "Tangled Clan," I'm told, and tangled he was, a spineless tumbleweed adrift in the wind. Once we were home, my mother told me to pack my things, which wasn't much: a mattress, a gym bag for my clothes and shoes, some toys I rarely played with, and my small stack of books from the school library. When we left the reservation, all our belongings had fit into the old GMC pickup we owned then, and packing up on that day had felt similar to how it felt today. We'd always been transient, ready to flee or move at a moment's notice. And I've always kicked myself for not somehow noticing my lack of care and stability. This isn't happening because we don't love you anymore or anything, Mom said, helping me pack. We must correct what's not been right. Okay, I said.

■ ■ ■

I went to live with my cousin who, in her early twenties, was pursuing a master's degree in mathematics and teaching as a graduate assistant at the state university in Flagstaff. Her responsible nature was due in part to our strict and thrifty grandmother, who had raised her while her parents vanished into their depression and the poison of its alleviation. I was her, in a sense; her fondness for me was not at all veiled. She had just purchased a newly built condo in a blighted neighborhood that was within walking distance of my junior high, and her ads for a roommate had come to nothing, so I filled the vacancy. Based on her experience with her own parents, she made an arrangement with my father and mother that entailed a monthly allowance of $150 from each of them, with the stipulation that if they missed or denied me these monthly payments, I would go to the authorities, maybe the school counselor, with a story of neglect and abandonment, which wouldn't be so far-fetched, so beyond the stereotypical situation of young minority parents ill-suited for heavy responsibility. In this way, I was beginning to understand how to pit expectation against the potential for profit, and in this way, I was truly assimilated. Father puffed out his chest, a bottom-rung rooster. We will renegotiate these payments, he said, when you turn sixteen, see if you're in need of money then too. Mother, with her impeccable posture, sat in a chair pursing her red-stained lips. And, she said, when you're eighteen, hopefully grown into a man by then, the payments will stop. For a year the payments arrived on time, then every other month, until they didn't arrive at all. My parents eaten up by their lives and the ravenous world.

∎ ∎ ∎

The stopped payments should have rattled me more or forced me to follow through on the threat of going to the police or Child Protective Services, but I didn't assume my parents had vanished with even a semblance of happiness. I knew they had desiccated in their own despair. With my share of the rent, utilities, and food costs suddenly my own, I was encouraged to find employment. You're on your own now, said my cousin. You have me,

I began to skip school, sleeping late into the afternoons, which forced my cousin to drag me from bed and into the shower one evening, and then plop me down in the living room, where a pizza sat steaming on the coffee table. I ate ravenously while she chewed slowly, deep in thought. She told me it was time I snapped out of it. I couldn't go on like this any longer because my clients would lose their patience and school would begin to pry. It's all right to be out sick a week, she said, in order to get yourself back together, but any longer than that and what you had before might not be there. She asked what might make me feel better again. I thought quietly, munching a slice, and answered that trips to the library had once been something I had looked forward to but had forgotten about since the departure of my parents. There had been, in those days, a single public library across town from where I lived with my parents and from where I now lived with my cousin. It was too far for me to walk, especially round-trip. When Dad still existed, he took me, I explained to my cousin. It was an activity that brought him happiness, at least as far as I could discern. He reveled in being away from Mom, acted childish and giddy, and would tell me off-color jokes. What do Hopis have that is long and hard? he would ask. I would shrug, eager for him to reveal the answer. Their last names, he would say, laughing as we sped toward the library. Once we were there, my father let me out at the front entrance, said he'd be back in two hours. Plenty of time for me to wander around and wonder at the stacks. He never returned on time, was always half an hour to an hour late, dizzy in his boots and flush-faced, shirt-half tucked, hair mussed, smelling like soured perfume and chlorine. My cousin nodded firmly, told me to finish eating and grab my shoes. She had an idea and wanted to know if I still remembered how to drive.

glow of an action-comedy flickering across her smiling face. In fact, she'd been a passenger in a car full of intoxicated friends, the driver included. A cop watched the vehicle drift and swerve and turned on his red-and-blue lights, pulling the car over. The friend who was driving failed the sobriety test, and because no one else was sober, either, they all spent the night in jail. My cousin walked across town the next morning, entered the front door sweating, her eyes sleepless and swollen. The drunk tank isn't a place you want to spend the night, she said, bunch of jaans and shit-kickers getting in each other's faces. She explained the possibility of losing her scholarship if the DUI had fallen on her. I've worked too damn hard for this shit for it to get fucked up, she yelled. This was, of course, before the days of smartphone apps and a choice of cab company, the only game in town being Settler Cab, which generally refused to pick up Navajos, or any other minority, especially if they were drunk and looking to get home. If they did happen to be allowed into a cab, these unfortunate folks would be dropped off on the outskirts of town, where they got either lost or picked up by the police, and in some instances froze to death. Women were often assaulted or raped, then abandoned to be gathered by the authorities, and their degradation continued further. Small mountain towns have dark underbellies, no matter how quaint, friendly, or liberal they seem. That's an illusion, built upon the death and destruction of an Indigenous population, hijacked and rewritten narratives that showcase the leather mask of progress, but from whose skin is the mask cut. The girls who had been in the car with my cousin were two sisters, also Navajo and related to me by clan, which compelled them to refer to me as their "daddy yázhí," their "little" or "small daddy," and the girl who had been driving, a half-Hopi, half-Navajo girl from my cousin's hometown of Tuba City who was like a dart, or a hummingbird, and was affectionally called Birdy. She and my cousin had played on the varsity basketball team together. Birdy, a point guard; my cousin, a small forward because of her solid frame and ability to box out bigger forwards and centers using her strength and elbows. The sisters, a year apart, had dominated their high school's volleyball squad, bringing home three back-to-back state championships. This crew of Native girls was confident, fist-throwing tough, sharp-witted, with vulgar senses of humor bordering on blasphemy, which made them the ideal role models and customers. There wasn't a narc among them.

■ ■ ■

My first chauffeuring gig went smoothly. My cousin rode shotgun, the sisters bent into the back seat with Birdy sitting bitch—that's what they called it, sitting bitch, for what reason I never knew. Pregamed and ready, with an elated, carefree buzz, they shit-talked rivals, whom I had never met and knew nothing about, the details of which engrossed me—"That skank snagged out this bull rider with a big-ass cold sore on his lip and then went and passed it to her man, she didn't even give a fuck," or "I'll tell you what, if we see those hoe-bags, I'm down to scrap, take off these hoops, I don't care if I fuck up my nails, stoodis"—rugged and rezed-out their infectious laughter and swagger, not giving one fuck whom they offended. This was something I wanted: camaraderie and confidence, disregard, happiness. It couldn't be real. I dropped them off a block from the main downtown drag around ten, when all the bars started hopping and everyone felt sexier and tougher, the air thick with big-dick energy, as the girls called it, and returned ten minutes after 2:00 a.m., parking in the shadows of a parking lot, alleyway, or street. Sometimes one or two of them found other ways of getting home or getting to someone else's home. Other times one or two people I didn't know piled in, and I hurried across town to be rid of the commotion and weight. A few nights my cousin appeared alone, her eyes furious, as if she'd been crying, her fists clenched and red with fighting. Two nights, no one showed up at all, though when I got home my cousin was there, asleep behind her locked door. And one time a man I'd never met came to meet me.

■ ■ ■

The night was a void when D tapped lightly on the window with the bulbous knuckle of his pointer finger. I cracked the window enough to prevent him from inserting it past the joint. Hey, my man, he said. The girls said you could give me a ride. He told me they had found some snags, that his friends had ditched him, and shrugged as if I could relate. I was trepidatious, but he named the girls, knew where each had gone to high school and what position each played, though he looked too old to have been in the same graduating class. My place is a couple miles south, near the interstate, he said. I'll pay you twenty bucks. D handed me a crisp note and sat quietly in the passenger seat as I drove. At some point he had me veer right onto a road that went past a new subdivision of prefabricated homes, where the city limits met Forest Service land and the streetlights vanished. We turned onto a nondescript dirt road and arrived at a log cabin, the hard bark logs stacked like bones, the trim on the windows and doorway painted sludge green. Dim light emanated from a window onto a white pickup parked askew. D grabbed my shoulder, sending shudders down my body. All right, my man, listen, he said. If I'm not back in twenty minutes, you leave and don't worry about me, okay? I nodded and he checked his watch against the digital numbers glowing blue on the dashboard and synced it to his timepiece. Twenty minutes, he said again, pointing to me and then to the treed and darkened road we had arrived on, and exited the car. An inescapable loneliness overtook me, and I began to weep. After ten minutes, I was able to calm myself and wipe away my boyish tears. The dread tightening my throat loosened and a death bell pinged in my ears. At the nineteen-minute mark, I was depressing the brake pedal and shifting into drive when D suddenly opened the passenger door and got in, having emerged out of the darkness like a ghost or time traveler. He smelled sour, hot, and chemically musky. Go, he said. I turned on the headlights and sped through the forest dark. D rolled down the window, closed his eyes, and leaned his head back so the cold night air blew through his black hair. I asked him where we were going, and he laughed. Straight to hell if you're not careful, he said. I'll tell you, just drive. The wind crested over him, the starlight contoured the shadows of his dark brown face, his slab of a body rested. I dropped him off at a large apartment complex at the edge of town that seemed to have sprung up overnight. Tall buildings like LEGO sets were clustered around lit pathways and manicured grassy amoebas. D punched my arm when he got out of the car, told me to tell my cousin to get me a pager and to give him the number right away. Here's an extra twenty, he said, to help you get that pager.

■ ■ ■

When my cousin's friends snagged boyfriends, they went out less and less, until they didn't go out at all. The younger of the sisters dated a White Mountain Apache guy who studied the biodiversity of soils and hoped to return to his nation to help develop an irrigation and farming enterprise. The older sister went through a string of bronc and bull riders, none of whom were good beyond a single night, until eventually she moved in with a calf roper who made his living as a boilermaker. She followed his power plant work to Utah and Montana until the two were never seen or heard from again. Birdy, the boisterous extrovert, got pregnant some months after the crew had dissolved and seemed to be devoting herself to some form of Christianity, not because she believed in a White and all-forgiving Jesus, but for the free and reliable childcare the church offered. I'd heard she still went out from time to time, though not at all with the frequency she had prior to motherhood, and loved her child more than anything in this soulless world. My cousin became despondent, spent long hours in her campus office working on teaching materials and equations of improbability. She wore pantsuits when she taught, instead of her typical jeans and polo shirts. She desired something new from life, and I felt, again, our time together ticking away.

■ ■ ■

I began spending more time with D. This time I was driving him to a rural residential area with the name of a failed cowboy western—Silver Bolero, Cowpoke, or Park Ranch—in a silver Lexus, its new smell intoxicating. The trunk held packages I wasn't supposed to know about. I was given directions to a barn, where I backed the car in, cutting the lights and engine, leaving D to wait in the darkness. Don't look back until the barn doors are closed, he told me. A different car would be brought to me, which I was to deliver to D's place, where I'd await a page with a number to call for directions on where and when to pick him up. At his apartment that night, someone knocked. I didn't answer, or move, right away, not until the second and third round of knocking became more insistent. I looked through the peephole, saw a head draped with platinum blond hair obscuring the face beneath it. The pager remained silent, so I released the dead bolt, and before I made the decision to open the door, a woman drifted in, at least it seemed that way to me, and went directly to the refrigerator and examined its contents without taking anything. She opened the freezer, removed a bottle of clear liquid, took two quick sips, and put it back. I dead bolted the door and sat on the couch. She asked if I was hungry and I nodded yes. We gotta get a pizza around here, she said. While she rose to look at the to-go menus stuck to the fridge with magnets, the pager buzzed, its little green light blinking alien-like. On the phone, D told me the woman needed to stay there for the night. Lock the doors and don't let anyone in, he said. I'll be back in the morning. Are you done with your business, sweetie? she asked. I'll order us a pizza and we can watch a movie. She was familiar with all the cable channels D had access to and complained that nothing new was ever playing, she'd seen every goddamn movie each channel ran. She reached into her large bag and pulled out a VHS tape with no label on it. I thought of something called snuff films and wondered if it was one of those, or maybe a dirty movie, and my heart raced in terror. When the pizza arrived, the woman inserted the tape into the VHS machine, and to my relief the title, *Sleepless in Seattle*, filled the screen. It was a thrilling experience, sitting on the floor beneath a blanket with her, eating pizza, laughing when she laughed. I felt like both the son in the film and the father, because I didn't know what fathers rooms, paged me, and awaited my call. When she returned to the table, the man had been apprehended by the bouncers and forced to wait outside. She was told she needed to leave as well but pleaded with the bar staff to let her wait inside until her ride arrived. Pulling up outside the bar, I saw the man leaning against a square brick pillar, hardly able to stay on his feet. The younger sister came rushing out of the bar and climbed into the passenger seat. As she did, the man pulled open the rear door and launched himself onto the seat, passing out immediately. One of the bouncers shoved the man's feet and legs into the vehicle with his foot and slammed the door. I drove without direction, concerned the man might wake at any moment. But the younger sister assured me that once the man was passed out, it was always for the night. She told me to head past the shit-kicker communities and go down into the desert lowlands north of the mountain. After an hour, she told me to pull over at a small, ancient-looking convenience store that was the last place you could purchase booze before entering the western end of the reservation. I parked by the near end of the building. She got out and opened the rear door and, using all her might, which was significant, pulled the man out of the back seat by his feet. His head clipped some part of the car and I heard him make a grunt-yelp noise, which was followed by the dull sound of a body striking the ground and a commotion of dirt. When she got back into the passenger seat, I sped back to town. At some point, she removed the man's wallet from her pocket, took out the cash, and handed it to me. Then she threw the wallet out the window. Rolled that fucking fucker, she said, tears at the edges of her eyelids. She guided me to her place, where she showered while I checked my pager and waited on the couch, flipping mindlessly through TV channels. I thought about calling

Silence

Tony's second wife was burning eggs downstairs in the kitchen, the hot carbon stench of embryonic poultry smothering him like wet foam. He listened to the muted clatter of her cooking and recalled previous years when he had been too hungover to rise for water or a piss. Years prior to his and Katie's courtship and marriage that seemed like only a few bad months filled with dank corners and shallow, blood-crusted wounds, but in truth were twenty-plus years flooded with booze and crass selfishness. These sober, better days he lay spread-eagle, sheets twisted around one leg, morning-wood with the give of thawing cookie dough in his hand. He tried pumping one out only to have it deflate, and thought on the dream he had awoken from: a campfire built by his parents on the far shore of a metallic moon lake, every direction returning him to the same spot endlessly, until he became aware of his dreaming and a truck of its making, if he could somehow turn around in the lucid loop and locate the keys. The lapping of dream water forced him out of bed for a piss and a smoke that would mask the smell of charred eggs wafting upstairs.

Sunday. Fibrous clouds clawed across the sky beyond the porch railing where Tony's Light 100s were left from last night. It wasn't a porch, exactly, but an easy solution to underbudgeting: the railing butted up against the exterior trim of the sliding door, which felt like a toddler cage that kept Tony and his wife from tumbling out. The mortgage was inexpensive, cheaper than the daily/weekly/monthly rate for one of the squalid units at the Elden Motor Inn along Route 66, rooms Tony rented out to a continual flow of drifters, traveling tradesmen, and ex-cons who made their stays on Flagstaff's eastside. He wasn't despicable, or greedy, for inflating his motel rates, but principled—he was a man of principles. Accommodating a stranger's suspicious needs or giving leeway to their misfortune only led to unresolved issues and unpaid bills, stresses that derailed his amateur corrido career. One day soon, he kept telling himself, he would hire a reliable full-time manager for the day shift. Someone like Devin, the night shift manager, who stayed alert reading science fiction books or painting small figurines with needle-tipped brushes for some highly involved tabletop war game, his passion and perseverance evident in each brushstroke and washing coat. Throwing your all into it, becoming it, *making* it your own blood, your own spit to spit, he thought.

When Tony's parents arrived in town from the south during the late seventies, Mexicans, Navajos, and various surrounding tribes gathered on weekends in a park below the observatory where Pluto had been discovered. As the town grew, whitened into a vacation destination through the eighties and nineties, the browns were pushed out and forced into their own redlined enclaves. Scraping out lives in dilapidation, working in kitchens, cleaning rooms, or hunched behind hedges manicuring nature's detritus, maintaining the mountain bustle. But god-fucking-forbid too many of them hang in the downtown gastropubs and fusion restaurants, hitting on the yoga-panted White chicks. The neighborhood of Tony's youth was now segregated from the dull heart of the tourist-dependent epicenter, coagulated with late-thirties adolescent bros and the fawns that trailed them.

Crisp outside air blew against Tony's bare skin. His nipples hardened and he pushed them in and they popped out over and over again. He twisted the cherry off his cigarette onto the pocked sidewalk below, flicked the butt past the chain-link fence separating his duplex from the overgrown lot next door. It was only a matter of time before the lot sold and the ground was broken to build cramped, low-rise studio apartments that would be advertised as one-bedrooms with a partition between where the bed went and the rest of the living space. A door no longer defined a room. He turned back inside, flopped face-first onto the bed, and began singing. The lyrics, or the intervals of them, were inaudible through the pillow and comforter. No one was listening anyway.

■ ■ ■

Katie skidded across the kitchen linoleum, slick with multiple layers of greasy film after tornados of cooking and half-assed attempts at cleaning it with an overused Swiffer pad. None of her gusto remained after six long days of keeping her clients' McMansions immaculate, her makeup melting off her face through the heat of the work. Tony had always told her that the foundation and blush she wore distracted from the lived, and real, features of her wonderful face: chin scar from hopping a fence in her adolescence, a nicked forehead from taking a spill during a high school cross-country meet. Features he had once met with the softness of his lips, but his kisses of late landed on the crusted corners of her mouth. A month had passed without any intimacy between them. No use shaving in a landing strip if he wasn't ever going to attempt to focus his descent on her, she thought. The guy before Tony had an insatiable appetite, which she had loved at first, being desired so much, whenever and wherever. Until it became the problem, she couldn't even take a shit without the guy trying to creep around the door and jam his dick inside her. With Tony she came most every time; his large, knobby phalanxes, which made playing chords easier, threw Katie into spasms when he fingered her. He could be attentive, take his pleasure in hers. Now he was like one of those matryoshka dolls that fit one inside the other, smaller and smaller. Katie knew he was in there somewhere, but she worried how tiny.

She toasted two slices of wheat bread, thinking, Son of a bitch, though she had never met his mother or father. Not even after their nuptials in the courthouse nearly a year back. Both of her parents had attended the after-party, neither staying too long, because it was dry, and booze was required for them to be in the same town. Her mother had worn a regal silver dress that day, bought by her new husband as a show of having remarried up. Her father managed to match a tie with a shirt that stayed tucked in until the secret bottle he nursed took effect and he disappeared to some hotel bar, where he likely disappeared more. She had no idea what Tony's parents were like, and probably wouldn't ever find out. He never offered anything more than that he'd lost touch with them some years before he and Katie began dating. The few times she did approach the topic, her inquiries were met with him leaving the room for the solace of his guitar or the house for quiet hours-long walks.

Katie sliced an avocado to go with her crispy egg whites, turkey sausage, and toast, doused it all in tomatillo salsa. She had made enough for two, set a place for her absent husband, and debated yelling for him to come down for breakfast or ascending the stairs, where she suspected she'd find him cradling his broken guitar, staring blankly at the wall. Instead, she held her breath to listen to what she determined was Tony's humming or mumbling, until the throb of her pulsing blood rang in her eardrums.

■ ■ ■

Tony had played a ramshackle gig the night before at an eastside bar a mile from his inherited motel. Some months before Katie arrived in his life, his parents had signed the property bond over to him and returned to Oaxaca. After a long life making it in the States, they wanted to spend their final years in their original home, where they also wished their bodies to be buried. Oaxaca, or any other part of Mexico, was a place blurred by the wavering heat of Tony's imagination. The closest he came to the border were the occasional trips to Phoenix he took with his parents on a Greyhound to visit family he hardly understood or cared to be around.

The Railroad Tie was a reputed Indian bar with a mixed clientele of Mexican and gritty White folk. Katie often joked that she couldn't always tell if any one of the patrons was a minority or just some dirty, sun-beaten White person, which made Tony laugh. He could always tell the difference. The sinewy hunch of a good old boy framer who subsisted on well liquor and cheap cigarettes talking of better days when he didn't have to work so hard to have to work so hard.

Tony's trio was sound-checked, ready to roll by six. Tony played rhythm and crooned while the bassist and lead guitarist he'd found on a back page listing sight-read from a mix of tablature printed off the internet. He dubbed the scrappy outfit Las Canallas de las Montañas. In addition to each player's wife or girlfriend, the audience consisted of a scattering of early-evening drunks and a table of pregaming hooligans shooting stick. Las Canallas de las Montañas played six covers, mostly standards, less complicated to play than contemporary hits. He'd need four to six more musicians, matching outfits, more talent than he possessed, and stronger songwriting capabilities to pull off any of the new tunes.

During the forced applause before the final song, one of the young hotheads, after racking a game of eight ball, shouted, "Can you putos play any current shit? Me cago en tus putas madres."

When unimpeded by insults or nerves, Tony's half-assed Spanish might go unnoticed beneath the cadence of elongated and emotionally strained words. In the six months he'd been attempting to compose his own music, he was able to conjure only third-rate rip-offs of his favorite tunes. And lyrics, forget it. He could barely rhyme *true* with *screw* and especially not in Spanish. He slurred, mispronounced, forgot a majority of the final song's lyrics, and after the heckler berated Tony further for being an old, half-assed wannabe Mexican, Tony threw his soda bottle toward the kid, and it shattered against the pool table. Before anyone was able to hold the heckler back, he caught Tony with a wild haymaker, causing him to fall and land awkwardly on his guitar, cracking the joint where the heel met the body.

Later, in the parking lot, Tony spoke with cops who didn't bother taking out their notepads. *Just another night at the Railroad Tie*, their indifferent postures seemed to say, *another dead end.* As they pulled away in their cruisers, Tony noticed a shadowy figure standing where the strip mall ended at an alley, though it was too tall and lanky to be the same punk-ass heckler. When he strode toward the figure, it backed away, and he thought he heard the sound of galloping, but it could have been the acoustics of the bricks in the darkness. He refrained from saying anything to Katie on the drive home, preferring the rattle of the car heater, and the mustard beam of the headlights cutting the cold, to any conversation.

■ ■ ■

Katie watched him patter around the kitchen in threadbare underwear, shaking and clutching handfuls of his beautifully thick black hair, cigarettes nestled precariously between his strong gut and the blown-out waistband. She leaned against the newly cleaned countertop, alternately sipping lukewarm coffee and ice water, waiting for the pack of smokes to be worked loose into the groin section of his shorts.

"I should've beat his young, cocky ass," he repeated, as if it might physically summon the hooligan to him there in the kitchen. He rubbed at the tension locked in his forearms and shoulders with the firm hands Katie had been wanting to make her flesh tingle red.

"Why don't you try pounding this ass?" she asked, guiding his hand there. She'd been waiting for him to come downstairs, waiting for this reflective rant, waiting to calm and quiet her husband's cracked sense of trust and safety.

Tony flinched, a sudden discomfort of his attraction, and relaxed a moment. He gripped her and pulled her against him, the toothpaste-and-cigarette heat of his mouth tickling her neck. She felt him grow against her abdomen, the corner of the cigarette pack poking her as she pulled his underwear easily off, guided him bare-assed to the couch, and let slide to the floor her workout shorts before straddling him, the urgency of their breathing in opposition to Katie's grinding rhythm until the tempo of both stalled and quit and Tony moved her off him, pulled up his shorts, and grabbed his pack of smokes on his way to the kitchen, where he stood mumbling an apology about being too distracted or something, his penis an embarrassed swell beneath the shield of his underwear.

Katie sat winded, throbbing. She smoothed and tied her disappointment up into a ponytail. She debated lighting a candle after Tony pulled a cigarette from the pack, but couldn't remember if there were any and made a note to buy some when she went out again.

"Open a window," she said. "We can try again later. I'm going to have a shower. Want to join me?"

Tony grunted, standing in front of the kitchen sink, blowing smoke through the open window, the brown slab of him muted against the light pouring in. He drew water from the faucet into a clean-looking glass and gulped it down.

In the hot steam of the shower, Katie imagined the viscous remnant of her husband running out of her, mixing with the water streaming across her legs and sliding down the drain. They had never discussed the potential, the possibility or probability, of a child or children. She never had a second thought about staying on her birth control, taking it as regularly and automatically as she went on her morning runs, as she drank glasses of water. This far into their forties, having a child seemed more burdensome, and not for herself or Tony but the child, who would grow with aged and less energetic parents, not to mention grandparents, who were fading away into new lives or who had already vanished. Perhaps that's why Tony's parents had left without saying anything. They had given up on his giving them grandchildren. Her mother had certainly given up.

"By the time you find a decent man to have a child with, I'll be as good as dead," she had said.

But Katie had never really wanted kids. She always believed herself to be a burden and the reason for her parents' diminished dreams and eventual divorce. She rinsed conditioner from her hair and shut off the water. There was still plenty of time to live yet, she thought.

Back in the living room, Tony sat fully clothed on the couch, a guitar Katie didn't recognize lying flat on his lap. It was old but well cared for, the deep red grain of the wood a mirrored storm of canyons, the rosette around the sound hole resembling a complex and mysterious language. The nylon strings looked like polished tendons or ligaments, the tuning pegs crafted of bone or ivory. It hummed, shaping the air around it.

"Where the hell did that come from?" she asked, wondering how long she had been in the shower.

Tony shook his head, drummed his thick fingers across the strings at the bridge, filling the room with a cavernous thrum. He positioned the instrument in his arms and played an E minor, which made every chord he'd ever played before sound like weak static, thin tin.

"There was a knock. A hard one," he said. "Just one hard-ass knock on the door. When I opened it, I heard a clacking noise.

Like hooves or fancy-ass shoes." Tony held the guitar up to her, an offering to make real the occurrence of this strange item.

Katie took the guitar by its neck and base, ran her hands across the solidness of its shape, the gloss of its polish. It was light, nearly weightless in her hands. The urge to play it overcame her, though she didn't know how.

"You didn't see anyone?" she asked. "Someone seriously just left you this guitar and ran?"

"Who says it's for me?

"Who the hell else would it be for?"

Tucked into bed that night with a biography of Mexico City, Katie listened to Tony intermittently strum chords without progression or rhythm. No melody or intention, just curiosity. She began to wonder how a city came to have a biography. A city couldn't write an autobiography, couldn't determine its fate or reflect upon its own shortcomings. All this was determined by its inhabitants who chose to bear witness, record, and keep the story of the place that kept them. Captured, overrun, or abandoned, the city was perhaps an orchestrator, not a storyteller. The eons of its layers and depths were a time signature for the digging ticktock of civilization. She wanted, then, the slow breathing of her stunted husband as he drifted into sleep, and despite the night terrors he sometimes had, she yearned to lie with her ear pressed against the mattress, her forehead resting against his spine to steady, steady, steady the rhythm of her breathing in a vain attempt to match her heartbeat with his.

■ ■ ■

The next night Tony unlatched his guitar case and removed the snapped carcass within. It dangled from his hand like a puppet as he walked to the open sliding door, where he pitched it into the empty lot. The hollow body thumped and the air went quiet. Back in the bedroom, he placed the reverberating new guitar into what felt like an old grave and shut the lid. After putting on shoes and a jacket, he drove to the motel and parked before a vacant room.

He peered into the void beyond the window, remembering the rotation of sitters he'd been left with as a child. Each with their reasons to keep him hushed. Sherri, a night shift bartender who went back to sleep after Tony was dropped off, the front and back doors to her apartment locked with a key from the inside, who dosed his whipped cream and hot chocolate with vodka so he passed out in front of the television until his parents picked him up. Grace, the oxygen-tank-wearing diabetic whose son, Angel, five years Tony's senior, coddled Tony unless he received a beating from his mother's bronze-colored aluminum cane, which in turn Angel took out his anger on Tony. And Trina, a seemingly levelheaded and mature teenager who played VHS movies with sex scenes so she and Tony could re-enact them later in the bedroom, his body and penis a doll she manipulated, derived pleasure from, and shared with her boyfriend on at least one occasion, so that nothing of Tony was left untouched. Nights, he hid in his closet, mouth stuffed with a shirt, the bedroom light left on to suspend the night terrors and auditory hallucinations wrecking his sleep, making him piss the bed. Voices whispering from the unlit hallway, a heavy black paralysis overtaking him then and into adulthood.

A progression of sharp tremolo aches panged Tony's stomach. He hovered outside the flesh of his body, its warmth and heft now a nothingness. He returned to his truck and reversed it without thought or intention, his muscles driven by need. The nearest drive-through liquor store was a quarter mile to the northeast, open until two in the morning. It was easy, smooth, and familiar, asking for a pint, then quickly correcting to a fifth of tequila, the crinkling sound of the bag around the bottle neck a soft reassurance, the rough paper folded beneath his sweaty palm an anchor easily dissolved. The cashier behind the small window bored beyond judgment.

Back at the hotel, Tony parked in the shadows cast by the glow emanating from the manager's office. Inside, Devin, the night shift guy, hunched over a sci-fi novel that was more cinder block than book. He jumped when Tony announced himself.

"Hey, no tiny men tonight?"

"Nah," replied Devin. "I painted what I had of the army I'm building. I'm saving up for a chief sorcerer and primarch. What brings you by this late?"

Tony shifted in place, ran a hand nervously through his hair.

"Was feeling restless at my pad. Thinking I'm gonna use number six as my jam space since it's on the end there. Write some tunes."

"Didn't your guitar get broken?"

"It did. But I've got a new one."

"Nice. I'll get you the key and mark it as indefinitely occupied."

Tony's heart crawled up his throat and his forehead began to perspire.

Devin returned with the key, his face creased with doubt and concern. "You all right, boss? You're looking a little clammy."

"No, no. I'm tranquilo, fine. Just a head rush. You wouldn't mind ringing the room in the morning when you leave? Make sure I'm awake before my shift."

"Not a problem, jefe. I've got you covered. Hasta la mañana."

"What?"

"See you in the morning, boss," said Devin.

Inside room six, Tony switched on all the lights. He took the blanket from the queen-size bed and hung it over the front window, leaned the mattress against the wall shared by the room next door, and dismantled the bed frame. Next he pulled the single chair from beside the small eating table into the center of the room. It wasn't so long ago that he'd done something similar in the house he rented with his ex-wife. Holed up in what was supposed to be the guest bedroom after a drunken fight. Throwing plates and beer cans, making Swiss cheese of the Sheetrock with his fists. Long and frequent benders leaving him useless and shaky for days after, until his wife left divorce papers and a note on the kitchen counter telling him she was gone for good. A song worth writing, perhaps. Nothing like the corridos about heartbreak beneath the moon's light or the arduous journey to woo back a beautiful woman. No, nothing like that. The songs in his head were ethereal compositions of his secret abuse or the anger that fissured his nerves whenever stress or uncertainty overtook him.

Tony sat in the chair, the guitar in his arms positioned to play, the unopened bottle of tequila next to his foot. He was too old and didn't know shit. His fingers made chords, all diminished. He strummed from the wrist, over and over, no idea where he was or what he was doing.

■ ■ ■

On the weekends leading up to the show, Katie had cleaned extra houses while Tony rehearsed in the duplex alone. He sang and played better when he thought no one was around, and Katie was touched by a swift sadness about never being able to hear the small brilliance of Tony's music. As her stack of travel books and imaginary trips grew, her desire to keep the duplex clean faded, and she spent the late afternoons and early evenings sipping water and wine, dog-earing page after page of foreign and domestic destinations, beachside resorts, and historic sites. In all their years together, she and Tony had never visited any place other than Phoenix. Hardly worth counting, since all they did was stroll through air-conditioned malls and guitar stores, always returning to Flagstaff the same night.

When she and Tony first met, Katie told her parents that he was a good man, not anywhere near perfect, but a good, kind man. She learned about his alcoholism and many attempts at recovery as the months passed and their love turned domestic. Tony installed timed light switches in her apartment, helped her unclog her shower drain, painted an accent wall in the kitchen, and always washed and dried the dishes when he stayed over. She drank in front of him until the anger and frustration of it caused him to erupt and he punched a hole in the wall he had painted, shattered a coffee mug on the floor, and left suddenly, only to return, weeping at her feet. After that she drank whenever he was out, stealing those moments for herself.

As Katie read, she created four potential travel itineraries: Paris, for not taking the travel-abroad opportunity with her high school choir. Edinburgh, for the wizard-boy movie locations and sexy accents. Montreal, for its cheaper flights and mess of cheese fries smothered in gravy. Mexico City, for its proximity and probability. If she ever got there, she thought, spent a little time, she could make a detour to Oaxaca. A two-night trip at the very least. It couldn't be impossible to track down Tony's parents. He must know their whereabouts, have an address stashed somewhere. But maybe she was *White*-girling it, something Tony would accuse her of: her wanting to help, even if it meant pushing.

Katie opened a browser on her laptop and booked a two-week trip to Mexico City: round-trip flight, a hotel close to Bosque de Chapultepec with shuttle arrangements, two museum passes, and dinner reservations at a Michelin-starred restaurant. She poured a third glass of wine and began to shelve and restack her travel books. In her euphoria, she decided to do a packing run-through of one roller bag and a backpack, like she had read about in her travel guides: items for mobility and variety that ensured one's pleasure while traveling without burdensome and needless possessions. The process felt freeing and natural, like she had been destined for it all along.

■ ■ ■

The tequila went down easy. A pinpricking shudder ran across Tony's skin. His chest became a sinkhole and his stomach turned hot and sour. He walked zombielike to the Railroad Tie. Inside, he stood unsteady at the bar, slurring a string of obscenities at the bartender, who said something like "No, not you again, you've done so well . . . I'm calling, I'm calling." Then the cold coarseness of the alley pavement on his face and a sheen of vomit leading away from it, the bilious scent filling his mouth and nostrils. His shirt was wet and torn from some unknown altercation.

In the darkened distance, a woman's voice called his name. He knew the timbre but couldn't recall from where. At the far end of the alley a hole had been cut in the gate portion of the fence. To escape the voice summoning him, Tony rose to his feet, staggered toward the opening, and fell through it.

On the other side was an abandoned mobile home, its busted-out windows patched with cardboard scraps and duct tape. The grass on the rectangular lawn around it was dead. Tony stood more firmly. A street curved into a smile before him with more mobile homes sitting like rotten teeth. Early-evening bats darted through the cones of streetlights, feeding on invisible bloodsuckers. There were no screaming delinquent children or entertainment systems droning movies or the nightly news. A few cars lined the streets, older models, late-seventies to late-eighties. The trailer park looked forgotten, discarded by elders long passed.

Tony walked along the road to his left and soon came upon a single aluminum home with its porch light on set among a cul-de-sac of ponderosas. He ascended the misshapen steps and knocked.

"That's not the home you're searching for," said a phlegmy voice.

Tony turned around to see a man, or a woman, who wore a baggy denim work shirt tucked into brown corduroy pants. A bulky knit cap was pulled low over their eyes, the wrinkled face coming to a blunt triangle below the cap. Its skin pulsed softly with luminescence.

"Who says I'm looking for something?" asked Tony.

"If you're wandering around here this time of night, then you're looking for something."

"Like what?" Tony said, descending the steps and spitting.

"Oh, come now, stranger. Tell me you can't imagine what happens in a place like here?"

Tony stepped forward and the person moved back quickly.

"A lot goes on in front of that bar and sometimes nothing at all."

"Are you the one I saw, then? The one who left the guitar?"

"Guitar? Maybe you have me confused with someone else, stranger? I'm not fit enough to leave this place. And I know nothing about guitars."

"Someone came to my house, left me a guitar." Tony moved forward once more, and the moved person backward again.

"A fortuitous gift. Accept it."

Tony had never fully explained the extent of his abuse to Katie, only hinted at his difficult childhood. Not at the hands of his parents, who had overworked themselves for his wellbeing, but of those his parents paid to take care of him. He had been born with a knotted umbilical cord and was deemed a miracle baby, while his mother had suffered complications from the birth and the removal of her ovaries, which made him the sole hope for the family line. His parents were ignorant of the abuse, as far as he knew, or lived in denial of it. And there it festered, Tony silencing it with booze that led to eruptions that hurt everyone around him. But he was feeding it music, too, not explicitly but subtly, perhaps, behind the chords he composed, the words he hadn't written yet. Why not accept the guitar as a gift and nothing more? Searching for answers, reasons, fostered regret and uncertainty.

"Hey, stranger," said the figure. "Sounds like someone is looking for you. But it's up to you if you want to be found."

"I'm feeling woozy all of sudden," Tony said. "I think I need a place to lie down."

The figure laughed and lit up a hand-rolled cigarette that smelled sweet and earthy.

"Get a little of this in you," they said. "It'll take all those pukey feelings away."

Tony took the smoke and dragged on it deeply a couple of

times. The tightness that had been cinched around his head loosened. He felt like a dandelion coming apart in the wind, the pain of his stomach and intestines releasing all around him.

■ ■ ■

The night was warm, and the mosquitoes were biting. Katie arrived to meet Devin at the Railroad Tie. Tony and the bartenders all went back, had history, even though they hardly acknowledged one another whenever Tony played gigs. There was much from that time in his life that was still unknown, and plenty of people willing to keep it that way. So she was grateful for Devin being the middleman in a time like this, no matter how much it stung.

"Thanks for coming," he said. "I locked up the office and hurried over here after I got the call, and then called you. However long it takes, we'll find him."

Katie hugged Devin, who seemed to be pulling away until she released him.

"No, thank you," she said wiping tears from her eyes. "You go in and talk with the bartender. I'll stay out here and see if I see anything."

Devin nodded and strode away quickly before disappearing inside the bar.

There were no cars in the parking lot, no reassuring visage of Tony's truck. Everything was a combination of monochromes: opaque night and gray asphalt markings, yellow streetlights reflected egg yolk in the vacant strip mall windows. She folded her arms, hunching her shoulders as if they might shield her neck and ears, and examined the covered walkway until her eyes stopped at the alley. There she approached the fence and called

Tony's name. She clawed at and shook the metal links of the gate. A small shadow appeared, followed by a taller one.

"Excuse me," Katie cried out. "Can you help me?"

"That's already been done," hacked the smaller shadow, now visible. It looked to Katie to be a small boy or dwarf of a man, and she thought its face resembled that of a shaved otter.

Behind the small person stumbled Tony, nearly blacked out for sure. Dark stains of vomit blotted his shirt. A peninsula of urine ran down his pants and she caught the scent of shit. My poor man, she thought. What have you done?

"This body yours? Found him dead in the street. Don't know how he got through. The gate is always locked. I'm the only one with a key."

The figure pulled a string from around its neck, on the end of which was a large gold key, much too fancy for the chain-link fence. Once the gate was unlocked, the small figure guided Tony across the threshold without crossing it. Tony wobbled into the alley and fell to his knees. He mumbled like a child terrified of some inexplicable monster. Katie hurried to him, knelt, and took him in her arms, kissing his head of greasy black hair despite his pungent odor. His body relaxed and his heft became hers.

"Thank you," she said. "How can I repay you? Is there anything I can do for you?"

The small figure locked the gate before speaking. "It's done. Don't come back here. Next time there will be no one. Nothing to find."

Katie blinked before replying, but the person was already gone.

■ ■ ■

The morning air was thick with coffee, the windows a blur of sunlight. Tony lay naked on the couch, a towel haphazardly draped over his genitals. Katie moved quietly through the kitchen, turned the faucet on and off, and put bread slices in the toaster. Tony sat up when she approached with a hot cup of black coffee and a glass of Alka-Seltzer.

"Drink these," she said, setting down the liquids and rubbing circles into Tony's back.

"How'd I get here?" he asked. "How did you find me?"

"Devin called me after the bartender at the Railroad Tie called him. I found you in the alley with some little person. Strange, if you ask me. It's kind of foggy in my mind. Anyway, Devin helped me bring you here and into the shower."

Tony sipped from the steaming cup, then swallowed the fizzing water.

"I'm sorry," he said. "I don't know what I was thinking. I don't remember anything after the motel. I don't know what I did. I'm sorry."

Katie embraced and rocked him.

"No, no. You didn't do anything bad. It's all okay. You did leave the door open, and the guitar was stolen. But we can get you another one. We can go somewhere to get you another one."

The two hugged tightly and found each other's mouths, both bitter and warm. The light from the windows wavered radiantly in time with Tony's anxiety and shame. He looked at Katie, who seemed changed. She wore new clothes with extra pockets, a material made for comfortable hiking, and her makeup was different. There was kohl around her eyes and something that made her skin dewy. When she smiled at Tony, her teeth were smooth and immaculate.

"I'm going to Mexico," she said. "I booked you a ticket but you're more than welcome to stay. I see that you're going through a lot."

She paused and kissed Tony. And she continued: "But so am I. In my own way. I need to do this, for me. I thought I also needed to do this for you. I was wrong about that."

"Mexico?" Tony asked. "What's there to find in Mexico?"

"Fucking guitars. Corrido singers. Who the hell knows? I'll be there and can help you through whatever you're going through. Just from there, not from here."

Katie continued to talk, Tony's head pounding with uncertainty and confusion. He leaned back on the couch and thought of how his ex-wife had vanished off the face of the earth, of how his parents might someday soon lie buried beneath the soil of an unknown graveyard in Oaxaca, and of his final night on earth, or at least last night had seemed so. Tony couldn't imagine the distance between Oaxaca and Mexico City, only the millions of undefined faces of those places and, emerging suddenly from that throng, the tentative smiles of his parents. Not smiling at him, necessarily, but for having made what they could of their lives and finally returning home.

He didn't know what Katie was saying when he interrupted her with a long kiss.

"I'll go," he said. "I'll go."

When he looked at her, he expected tears, but Katie only nodded.

"Okay," she said. "I'll show you how I packed. I intend to come back with more than I'm taking."

Katie hugged Tony so tightly he couldn't move. We'll be leaving, in a few days we'll be leaving for Mexico City, he thought, excitedly. And then Katie walked away from him to the upstairs bedroom, her shoulders sturdy, straight, and confident, like she was already gone.

Before the Burnings

Part of Karl's night custodian job was to incinerate the monthly shipment of test subjects that arrived through a tunnel, half a mile away, on Forest Service land, to a secure basement beneath Research and Development, where a freight elevator ascended to surgical rooms. Karl's only contact with the discards came after the large storage freezer had been filled to its ceiling and he was forced to dismantle the frosted wall of red plastic bags— black biohazard flowers folded and partially exposed—then cart the subjects and heft them into the cremation furnace. When he was hired, Re-Dev's head explained to Karl that this process was the most ethical, efficient way to dispose of the strays, rabbits, and coyotes that a statewide euthanization project abundantly provided. Some of the human remains Re-Dev received were organ-donor accident victims, but most were inmates and ex-cons who, after having maintained a semi-consistent good behavior status while locked up, were granted the opportunity to donate viscera or their entirety to science in exchange for time off their sentences. Each organ fetched seven days. A whole body, seven years. Bodies that became the property of science.

At first, the secret incinerations mattered little to Karl. Twenty-two years old, with a high school education, he wanted decent on-time pay that didn't require an early clock-in and afforded him the leniency and solitude to rock out to metal music cassettes on his Walkman. When HR demanded that he comply and sign two secrecy agreements—one regarding the facility's incineration and disposal of animals and inmates, the other concerning the secrecy of the secrecy agreement—Karl, without hesitation, scribbled his signature. Although some weeks after this, it was Jonas the anesthesiologist who suggested to Karl that if he was asked what the company he worked for did, he should answer that it manufactured micro-thin moisture barriers for extreme-weather active apparel and a noncarcinogenic hard plastic alternative. Never mention the company's unpublicized medical research, despite its unrivaled advancements in developing replacement arteries, synthetic blood vessels, joint cartilage, and breast implant sacs.

Karl listened to Jonas relate these facts and advice as unconsciously as he had followed him out of the building in the evenings to smoke, taking note of the access code Jonas entered for a side door that exited onto a small concrete pad next to a high-tension fence hung with No Trespassing signs. Outside, as the temperature fell, Jonas blabbed about the day—who was fucking up, who pulled their weight, who had never shown up without explanation again. These small conversations eased Karl's initial doubt about having to veil his secondary task. Jonas was above him in the hierarchy, and it was easy to talk to him about the uncertainty this new territory brought.

■ ■ ■

Three months deep—Karl nodded solemnly as Jonas spoke of Re-Dev's eminent production of a replacement esophagus and the overflowing freezer, felt a hard pang in his lower stomach. The surplus was kept in Jonas's smaller refrigerators, intended for sedatives and anesthetics. This violated protocol and national regulations, though there were no complaints thanks to Jonas's deletion of all paperwork concerning the existence of the improperly stored waste.

"I'm running low on anesthesia," said Jonas. "The docs are real close to having that esophagus working right. The recipient only needs to live two weeks with enough signs of recovery before it's certified production-ready. That's why you have your work cut out for you in the incinerator this week."

"They're making a dog esophagus?" asked Karl.

"No, dipshit. There's no money saving canine life. Dogs are just what've been available. You ask me, it's because of all the snowbirds overburdened by their money and pets. Primates cost too much and PETA's all over that. And getting a human cadaver with a neck is one in twenty-five. This company should really look into where all those disappeared, deported illegals end up. There could be some real money in that."

Re-Dev's stipulation with receiving human cadavers was that they got no more than half a body, a quarter of which was allocated to other research facilities or the state universities, so as to maintain an overall air of humane, scientific concern.

"So the docs aren't sure if the esophagus will even work on a human?"

"Sure they're sure," said Jonas, flicking his cigarette, exhaling smoke. "Parts are parts. The thing's just got to live the two weeks and then we'll start turning them out in all sizes, using coyotes, dogs, and whatever as templates. Hopefully we'll get donated a human neck. But if we really require one, one can be got."

Jonas rubbed his thumb and index finger together, stubbed his smoke on his shoe bottom, and placed it in his shirt pocket. Karl kept his extinguished cigarette as well. Both wanted to avoid any questions that might be raised by the heads if too many butts lay strewn about the doorway, as if this evidence of human activity were unsanitary and bothersome. Back inside, Karl flushed his down the toilet.

Before Jonas left the building, he asked Karl if he ever mentioned their conversations to anyone, a question he'd asked once early on, and which now seemed to Karl to be a formality regarding the sensitive knowledge Jonas had shared about the overflow of dog carcasses.

"I don't say shit," said Karl.

"Cool, cool. I only ask because of the nightmares I get being around all the testing. Sometimes it doesn't make any sense and other times it's perfectly clear."

"It's the hacked-up animals in bags that gets to me. Probably, I think, because there're so many of them and I can't tell one piece from another."

Jonas nodded without looking at Karl, walked away without saying goodnight.

Karl continued through his shift, sweeping floors, doubting that the night would go smoothly. He was indecisive about what metal genre might complement the stripping of the office hallways, which needed to have two coats of wax reapplied before Friday's scheduled burn. Previously, he'd decided on stoner rock for bathrooms, hair metal for sweeping and mopping, Euro-thrash for emptying garbage, and funeral doom for restocking. But since he'd been hired, he had never once had to strip the floors, especially during the week of a burn. So he mixed the stripping solution and switched out the polishing pad on the buffer to the abrasive black one and decided against listening to any guttural-vocal metal with lyrics about carnage, corpses, or satanic ritual and chose, instead, historical metal about medieval heroics—syncopated triplet riffs, clean operatic vocals—all of which kept his mind focused on his date with Angela and off the number of days left until the burning.

❚ ❚ ❚

Two weekends earlier, on the second Saturday of September, at a party hosted by his roommate, who insisted they call each other bro-mates, Karl fantasized once more about losing his virginity. Twenty-two pressed him. He believed his maturity level to be higher than it was, each drink bolstering his confidence. He no longer needed to hold out for the right chick. What really mattered was being ready at the right moment, anyplace, like he'd heard from friends who consistently found their way into the bedrooms of more than a few girls, or so they claimed. Armed with a proximal knowledge of hooking up and a woman's anatomy, thanks to his stack of porno magazines, which rivaled his comics, Karl visualized smoothing his hands along curves, the varying densities of flesh. From those crinkled pages, collaged into memory, he was certain he could seek out pleasure, take swift action when presented with a woman's naked body.

Karl hadn't noticed Angela noticing him—inebriated, he had stood spread-legged, air-picking bass lines to Iron Maiden songs, his pointer, bird, and ring fingers fluttering in time to the music while his left hand crab-walked across invisible frets.

After he jumped out of his metal-bass stance, he saw her—

black dress made of layered lace, which made her brown skin darker, more erotic in its unfamiliarity. Karl had never thought of a Navajo girl sexually, though he'd encountered plenty in high school. He'd always sought the attention of White girls, who shared his skin tone. But what he hadn't known then was that the musical preferences of these Navajo girls might have afforded him the opportunity to rock out to an album in a room, in a house, with parents absent. The chance that during a dramatic metal ballad, Karl and the melanin-enriched girl might lean close, feel the heat of each other's mouths, the motion of their bodies, and at the solo they would kiss, follow an arpeggio toward the floor.

Locking eyes with him, she crossed the room, said, "Hey, I'm Angela. You're Karl, aren't you?"

"That I am," said Karl, bowing slightly—scared shitless for having exhibited so much false bravado.

Angela told Karl she'd heard of him, of his guru knowledge and that his pantheon-like room housed an array of metal CDs, cassettes, and posters, his recommendations like those of an oracle. She was impressed he played bass with his fingers and not a pick, which Karl agreed was how real bassists rocked the instrument. Angela told him that she didn't consider herself a musician, though she'd taken piano lessons as an adolescent, but more of an aficionada—a rogue authority, she liked to think. She loved listening to metal, attending shows, and discovering innovations within the genre. Her favorite band was a Swedish group that mixed black metal with Sweden's folk standards. Karl admitted they were in his top ten, definitely top five of the European bands, then stalled for words.

The two stared at each other silently. The white noise of the room reverberating around them.

Finally, Angela said, "That's a pretty badass shirt. Judas Priest?" Karl's excitement blushed over his face. His shirt was thread-bare, the silk-screen print mostly disintegrated. Angela must have owned the *Painkiller* album: the image was of a molten city silhouette in a craggy valley beneath a burning sky, the blue exhaust of a dragon motorcycle with saw blade wheels being ridden by a steel angel-skeleton. The only parts that remained on the shirt were the blue above, the red below, and remnants of silver.

"Holy shit," said Karl. "You can tell who it is? That's awesome."

"Hell yes. It's a *fave*. Track three, the way the vocals fluctuate between the speakers at the beginning rocks."

"Totally. Totally."

Silence again.

After a stream of beers and an array of false-start conversation topics, Karl, unintentionally abrupt, asked Angela for her number. She'd been relating her thoughts regarding the legal battles that local tribes were having with ski lodge owners, who'd decided to make artificial snow from reclaimed water. Drought had made the winter's precipitation poor, and the lodge had opened for only a week the previous season, but that was not reason enough to disregard the mountain's spiritual and sacred significance. After Karl blurted his question, Angela told him that talking more now might prematurely skew her first impression of him; he was wasted, and she feared he'd turn into an asshole. She preferred to learn about Karl in a more coherent setting, so she wrote her number on a sheet of purple paper in white ink. Karl poked at it stupidly, aware of his gone sobriety.

"It was nice to finally meet you," said Angela. "Give me a call whenever you want." She turned to leave, hesitated, and added, "Don't wait too long."

Karl mumbled that he wouldn't and attempted to bow again, nearly ramming her into the wall. She caught the stout softness of him awkwardly and just in time.

Angela left the party alone, though Karl thought her friends might have exited ahead of her. Her faint lavender scent hung about the air as Karl watched her ass roll beneath her dress, and, suddenly aware of the supple shape of her back, he felt giddy with possibility and horniness.

Later that night, after forcing down a couple of shots and beers with his buddies for scoring her number, Karl puked until he felt thinned, shaky. Aided by the walls, he staggered to his bedroom and rifled through his porn stash for pictures of curvy, Rubenesque girls with dark skin, brunet hair. Bodies unlike those he encountered at work. The few he found, easily over-looked among the large quantity of blondes, didn't compare to Angela's smooth, clear complexion—her natural, unaltered beauty. After an overly lotioned effort, Karl came into a tissue, drifted into vacuous sedation. Passed out, magazine open, his body spread across the bed.

■ ■ ■

Two days before the burning, the temperature dropped to below freezing and a hard, dry wind blew pine needles from the for-est floors into the streets. Monday's and Tuesday's stripping had gone smoothly. Though there was one instance when Karl had tried forcing the buffer too much against its rotation, causing it to buckle, and was slammed into the wall until he released the handle-throttle. Fortunately, he hadn't slipped on the slick mess of stripping chemical and coagulated wax. His mind had drifted toward recollections of his and Angela's first date: coffee. The unfamiliar faux posh café that sold overpriced, burned coffee, and was filled with college students bent over textbooks. Angela had teased him for waiting ten days to call, and for making their date on a weekday during her lunch hour, which helped her know what he was or wasn't expecting.

Stiffened against the weather, Karl expressed his excitement to Jonas during their customary smoke. Knowing that Jonas would think him a fool for the logistics surrounding the date, Karl described Angela's ample body, the tempting softness of her flesh.

"Man," said Jonas, "I love women with curves. There's so much you can do, you know? Bam. Bam. My wife had curves once. Now . . . well, gravity's no joke."

Karl was sure he knew what Jonas meant about there being so much that one could do with a woman's curves but wasn't certain how one came to be able to do such things. Not a single one of the free clips he streamed on his computer in the dark of his room offered any idea of how to enact such sexual experiments, how a woman got a guy off with the folds of her body. Even though Karl was inexperienced, he wasn't foolish enough to believe that two people started fucking each other as a result of a guy delivering packages, buying shoes, helping change a tire, or being caught peeping a neighbor.

"Yeah," said Karl. "There's tons to do with her. Anyway, I asked her to a concert down in Phoenix. Her favorite band, my treat."

"That's it. That's the ticket right there, man. That's potential for head in the parking lot. You're in." Jonas gazed off into the treetops, most likely recalling a memory of his wife during the days when they found each other sexually enticing.

"So how'd the date go otherwise?" asked Jonas.

Angela studied Indigenous sovereignty rights, would have

her BA in a year, then pursue a master's. She spoke broken Spanish and was honing her Navajo with advanced language classes. Karl had said he knew Navajo, raised his hand, palm forward: "Yah tah hey." Angela curled her lips, distrust; the slow sway of her head, disappointment. He had pronounced it incorrectly—his way was offensive, ignorant—it was said, "Yá'át'ééh." Karl was defeated, annoyed. She told him Navajo was difficult and asked him to say, "Łíį'," which meant "horse." Karl's uncoordinated mouth butchered it—a heavy lisp and weak duck honk. Angela laughed, reassured him no one got it right their first twenty times. He attempted the word again. She giggled more. So he asked her to the show—he'd drive, they'd stay the night. She agreed quickly, but only if they went on a second date before the concert.

Jonas stared blankly at Karl, his cigarette long stubbed out, a fresh one resting between his lips.

"You came off sounding like a real asshole, man. You're lucky this girl's into you or you'd have blown it there. Shit, even I know how to say hi in Navajo. Being from around here and not knowing at least that, you've got to be one dense son of a bitch."

"I was trying to make a joke. I was nervous."

"Well, you got by. Next time you hang out, ask her about her clans. That's real important to Navajos. That'll get her attention, show her you're interested and not just a dipshit. Then bam, bam. Like I said."

"Clans, huh?" Karl asked, his gaze downcast. "I'll remember that."

When Karl looked up, Jonas was down the hall, rounding the corner. He'd left his second cigarette burning on the concrete pad. Karl thought the rings beneath Jonas's eyes were darker than usual, his speech trembling from lack of sleep. The nightmares must have been affecting him; one round of tests had been completed and others were soon to begin.

Karl stamped out the ember, picked up the remains, and went back to work.

With the hallways stripped, he mopped on a neutralizing agent, which primed the floor for new wax. When he finished, he walked out to his truck, smoked another cigarette, and opened the glove compartment to extract his one non-metal cassette: Billy Ocean's *Suddenly*. It wasn't mixed in with the rest of his tapes, because he saved it for special occasions. The last and only being a year ago when he had parked on the hilltop overlooking the westside of town after a girl he had been friends with in high school moved off to the city, leaving the knowledge of his crush alone with him.

Karl returned to the building and fast-forwarded to the title track. He lined his mop bucket with a trash bag, poured the wax in, opened a fresh mop head, and spread the opalescent glow slowly, delicately. When he finished, he looked across the translucent floor and thought that no one else would know the amount of dirt he had to remove so the surface appeared untouched, untarnished.

■ ■ ■

Nightmares: screaming rabbits sliced open, electrodes attached to their organs; a pile of dog body pieces writhing, whimpering; halved human in motion, torsos crawling with one arm or both, the bottoms walking; the freezer a flood of flesh; the incinerator burst, contents escaping, aflame.

It was Thursday, one day before the burning.

Karl woke exhausted, a hot metallic scent in his nostrils; depleted mentally, shallow with the guilt of his numbed, reddened cock dripping on sweat-dampened sheets. After the nightmares, he had succumbed to the momentary relief of masturbation, the act plunging him into a meaningless depression. But today he looked forward to more than a self-forgiving shower.

Yesterday, Angela had called during her lunch hour, his first hours awake. He sat in worn boxers at the kitchen table with cereal and coffee. Angela rambled on about the dynamics of her office—everyone's nicknames, coffee preferences, music. She told him there wasn't anyone, not one single pop-music-listening drone, who could show, let alone appreciate, heavier music. Karl agreed through mouthfuls of cereal and coffee that it was always difficult to find metal allies, especially in the workplace. He mentioned that his coworker Jonas had once said that the technicality and stamina seemingly required of metal were somehow defeated by the unintelligible, caveman vocals. Angela agreed that metal's brutal expressions of pain made it a pariah. She thought Karl was a man unafraid of human darkness—of a crumbling world vision. She found it attractive, said she felt closer to him. It was in that moment that Karl, half-awake and vulnerably sitting in his undies, forgot that losing his virginity had ever been an issue and told Angela he was happy just to have met her. Though it sounded trite, it didn't feel forced but genuine. Emotion stripped of intention. They hung up after making a date for the approaching Saturday, a day off for both, a week before the anticipated concert.

At work that night, the atmosphere was hectic and tense. Surgical technicians and doctors rushed through the hallways, in and out of doorways. They were ghosts in their cotton booties, left no prints on the new wax.

At 10:00 p.m., two hours before Karl's shift ended, Jonas appeared draped in two lab coats, the one beneath splotched with maroon stains. He stood pale, a victim of insomnia, but rigid, sturdy in the shoulders.

"Put up whatever you've been doing," he said. "We've got to get the incinerator going early. A shipment we can't use arrived. We need to get all the bags out of my refrigerators. The stuff in the main freezer can wait until tomorrow, but this needs to be done now."

Head sunk into his neck, Jonas disappeared through a door.

Karl's heart beat hard enough to rattle up and out of his throat. He hadn't really been working since finishing the floors, but airbassing a broom.

Inside the incinerator room, he put on thick rubber boots and a gray flame-retardant coat, scrub cap, and hard hat. Jonas, clad in the same safety gear, pushed a cart of large, red-bagged discards alongside a technician, who, as soon as the cart was close to the incinerator, rushed away.

Jonas lit a cigarette, the hollows of his face deepened.

"Let's get these going first. I've prepped the thing. It should be ready after this smoke. Want one?"

"We can smoke in here?" asked Karl, taking the cigarette from Jonas.

"Who's going to know? There aren't any fire alarms or cameras. It's just you and me in here until we're finished."

"Whatever you say," said Karl.

They began by flicking their smokes into the fire, then six or seven arms, a few legs, and a halved torso. Karl couldn't discern skin color, only the blurs of tattoos, some in Spanish. His mind was blank; his pace matched Jonas's. Not until they lifted the larger pieces at the bottom of the cart did Karl pay close attention: a torso with an arm, a couple of heads, the bottom half of a woman, hips to left leg, the right ending at the knee. The smooth slope of the crotch sent Karl, weak and nauseated, to his knees.

Jonas tripped as the weight of the load shifted.

"Fuck," he said. "I twisted my ankle. You've got to keep it together, man. There're just a few more. Don't look at it."

Jonas quieted. Karl watched firelight waver and shadow his face, thinking he might vanish. Some moments later, after a wordless nod, they threw in the remainder of the cart, and then emptied the smaller refrigerators of the undocumented waste. It all took an hour. But Karl waited while the incinerator cooled so he could push the ash into a rear compartment, using a long brush-squeegee, bag it, and toss it into the Dumpster.

When he returned home at two thirty in the morning, Karl wanted to call Angela—wanted her voice, her presence. But as he stared at the phone, he recalled the female leg and torso and looked away. Curled up in his blankets, he fought sleep until it overtook him.

∎ ∎ ∎

He woke Friday with only an hour to spare—bedding thrashed to the floor—a painful hard-on, the urge to release tainted with nightmare images of Angela sectioned. He tore through magazines, hoping in vain to find some spread, the right girl, but gave up. Overwhelmed and shamed, Karl hurried to get ready.

The phone rang.

He lifted the receiver, his voice weak in his throat. Instantly, Angela asked if anything was wrong, said he sounded upset. He said he'd overslept, was groggy, and had worked late. He apologized for not having time to chat; she responded that it wasn't an issue and wondered if he could take a break later. She'd bring coffee; they'd smoke. Yes, he'd call, they'd meet—it definitely sounded awesome. Before they hung up, Angela asked once more if Karl was all right. Of course he was, work was just intense—the break would be a relief.

Karl drove to work in absence of attention to surrounding traffic; his cigarettes; enough sleep; his duffel bag and Walkman, which, uncustomarily for him, were placed at the foot of his bed—forgotten for the first time, his mind minus the tunes that made his evenings pleasurable.

At work he did the basics: emptied trash cans, spot-cleaned floors, restocked and wiped down the bathrooms. He wanted to dash away and retrieve his music but didn't know when Jonas might ask him to begin the night's incineration. So he debated silently, even sat in his truck without starting it, only to return to the building. Inside, his mind burned under the buzzing fluorescent lights. His throat dried with waiting and his eyes tricked him with shadows scampering around corners, darting around the room's peripheries.

At ten to nine, Jonas appeared. Stringy hair slicked back, black stains on his neck from a clumsy dye job. He wore a gray corduroy suit, frayed at the cuffs and hems. He limped. The clack of his polished dress shoes made an unnatural rhythm.

"Karl, where are your headphones?" he asked.

"I slept in and forgot them. What's with the suit? And what happened to your hair?"

Jonas shot his hands out like a preacher, the sleeves of his blue plaid shirt bunching around the cuffs, and tugged at the lapels of his jacket.

"Meetings, man," he said. "Progress has been made. That's all

I can say. You were a real help with all that stuff last night. That stays between us and this building. I know I don't have to explain it to you. Smoke?"

Jonas extracted a half-empty pack from his suit coat.

"No. I'm good," said Karl.

"You're good. Okay. I came to tell you that you're on your own tonight. The bags are all small. It'll just take a little time." Jonas smiled. Karl had never seen him smile, at least not with all his teeth, which sat like chipped, blackened bricks in his mouth.

"You should get started if you want to get out of here," said Jonas.

"Right."

Karl's gaze dropped to the floor as Jonas clacked away. He turned before vanishing.

"Remember," he said, "this doesn't always make sense. But what needs to be done is clear."

He rounded a corner, his injured steps growing fainter, then silent.

Weighed down by the heavy coat and boots, Karl preheated the incinerator, wheeled a cart to the main freezer, and filled it—migraine smell of frozen plastic and fabricated frost. A few bags tore but nothing spilled, the chunks frozen solid. He tossed the discards into the flaming mouth, their weight bearable compared with last night's sudden arrivals. He even back-shuffled and threw in a few of the bags quarterback-style. When the oven was filled, he latched the feed door, waited for the contents to burn to ash. He estimated five loads remained and that he'd be done by three or four in the morning, much later than he expected. He lumbered out of the room, unlocked the first office he came to, and dialed Angela's number.

"I was hoping you'd call." The pitch of her voice high with excitement.

"Come as soon as you can," he said. "I need to see you."

"Okay," said Angela, unsure. "Is everything cool?"

"Yeah, work is really fucked. I could use someone."

"Well, just say so. I'm leaving now."

Karl waited outside, thinking of Jonas—his limp and his clacking shoes, the dyed black hair that melted off his head. The only aspect of his appearance that was formal enough for a supposed meeting had been the footwear. Everything else was mismatched, ill-fitting. Karl drew uncertain conclusions as to why and where a late-night meeting would take place. From all the shit he'd heard about the test subjects and their origins, he had assumed the meeting would be private, and who'd want to be publicly seen with someone as eccentrically dressed as Jonas had been?

He stood before the nondescript building as smoke ghosted above it and disappeared into the night sky. Some moments later, his bulky, misshapen shadow was thrown onto the building's wall as headlights appeared behind him and then cut off.

"What are you wearing?" asked Angela. "And what the fuck is that weird smell?"

She wore purple leggings, a faux leather skirt, and a corset top under a sheer sweater that was actually only the sleeves part of the sweater with a small amount of the back.

Karl faced her; her excited smile fell to worry.

"Have you slept?" she asked. "You look ill. Do you need me to take you home?"

Karl shook his head no. "It's this job," he said. "I can't do this shit. I don't want to do this shit."

"It's fine. You don't have to be a janitor. I'm sure you can find a different job."

"Custodian."

"What?"

"I'm a custodial technician."

Angela smiled at his failed humor, pulled her cigarettes out.

"No," said Karl. "Later. Come inside with me first."

Through the reflective-glass entrance, down nervous hall-ways, they came to the maw of the burning room. Before opening the door, Karl told Angela that nightmares had emptied him of sleep and that worry churned deep within him. She didn't understand completely but sensed the trouble.

"Just don't hate me," he said.

"No, no. Whatever it is, it's not your fault. Where are we?" Her uncertainty increased to fright, preparation for confronting the unknown.

Karl stood without answering, pulled the door open, and said, "I wanted to ask you about your clans. What do they mean?"

Angela stiffened, became guarded. "Basically, they define Navajos. They're the pieces of our ancestral makeup."

"Pieces," said Karl.

"Yeah, well, the parts of my parents and their parents and their parents. They keep our bloodlines pure, among other things. Why do you ask?"

"No reason," he said.

Inside the room, the maelstrom eye of the incinerator trembled orange-blue; the heat pressed the surrounding darkness onto them. Angela was drawn to the glow, a dizzied insect. Karl led her through the room to the door of the freezer.

"Here, this is it," he said. He placed his hand on her lower back, which felt cold from being outside, withdrew it quickly, the sensation reminding him of bagged bodies. But Angela was softer, alive. He returned his hand and urged her forward.

The red-bagged wall of mangled animals drew tears from Angela's eyes. She shook her head, pulled a small tan leather pouch from her purse, pinched some of its contents, and placed them in her mouth, muttering inaudible words. Her stunned expression hovered somewhere between fear and sacrilege. Karl thought to ask what was in the pouch, what it meant, but suspected he wouldn't understand anyway, so said nothing.

"I can't be here," she said. "I can't look at this."

Angela retreated from the freezer, saw once more the incinerator, and turned around to face Karl again.

"What's fucking happening here?"

Karl shuffled toward her, blabbered words about the testing, secrecy agreements, Jonas, the nightmares. He told her he'd been ignorant of the animal and human deliveries when he was hired. He'd learned to do this work, become patient through the burns. But he couldn't handle it any longer. And without music to distract him, the drone of the work had manifested the panic of his nightmares. He sagged to the floor and rested his head in his hands.

"Karl," she said, "I can't be here. I'm not entirely traditional, but Navajos don't mix the living with the dead. I mean, I shouldn't even be around people who handle the dead. I need to leave."

Karl, certain he'd offended and frightened her, didn't offer any comforting words. Asking her here had been a mistake. Angela rushed out the door and into the hallway, paced, unsure which way led to her escape. She hugged herself, which made her breasts bulge, her cleavage deepen. Karl, despite his apprehension, felt his cock grow, its warmth against his leg a reminder of temporary relief. But then he went flaccid, knowing that his hands had sent so many of the dead through this place of the discarded and forgotten.

Karl attempted to speak but only squeaked. Words piled up in his throat. Angela demanded he show her the exit and followed him at a distance to the front of the building. Out in the freezing darkness, she shivered, and Karl, relieved to be free of the room and building, moved to warm her with his arms. But she stepped away, her eyes shock-wide, her posture one of fear.

"Listen," she said, "I don't want to judge you, but I don't understand any of this. I wanted to be your friend and I've really started to like you, but what is this? What the fuck are you doing here?"

He didn't have an answer and said so. Her shoulders were hunched in frustration. Karl, moved by panic, seeking his own comfort, stepped in again to hug her, and grazed the side of her breast. Angela would have thought it was inadvertent if he hadn't slowed in withdrawing his hand, allowing it to stay a second too long. She stared at him vacantly.

"What the fuck is wrong with you?" she asked, shoving him to the ground.

Karl lay motionless, told Angela he'd really began to like her, too, hoped she'd understand and help, but didn't know how she could, exactly.

Angela kept herself from crying, told him with some amount of anger that she would be in her car while he decided what to do. If he decided to quit, she'd wait; if he stayed, she'd go. And after that, she wasn't sure what would be left between them.

Back inside, Karl filled a cart, pushed it to the incinerator, and threw in a bag with what looked to be rabbit pieces. It took the flame, popped, and smoked. He thought it smelled of burned fur, meat cooking, but wasn't certain. For a second Angela's scent materialized in his nostrils—the warmth of sex, a body that gave, responded. Exhausted, sweating, he removed his hard hat and scrub cap, threw them in, then the heavy coat and boots. They smelled unfamiliar. He'd never burned clothing. He thought of the music that usually filled his evenings, his soundtrack to this artificial funerary pyre, and how the heaving oven now felt like silence. Standing before its flames, he became a silhouette, a shape making its way toward light, or away from it.

Usefulness

We spent the day rolling an abandoned school bus, spray-painted pink by a previous occupant, down a hill of loose black cinders and into a clearing at the western edge of Otter's land. With a chain saw he had cut to length a couple of old railroad ties that he had lifted from a landscaping gig we had recently finished, and secured them to the steel grille guard on his work truck with baling wire. The oiled oak ties would help distribute the weight of the bus through the truck's chassis, avoiding damage to the radiator and engine. After sitting vacant for nearly a year, the bus was a haven for spider nests and small vermin. Gutted of its green vinyl benches and rubberized flooring, it had been outfitted by some hack with a seating area, a fold-down table for meals, a countertop with cabinets and a sink, closet space, and a sleeping area. None of it had been secured with the correct hinges or hardware, nothing leveled or squared. The building material was all scavenged but not refinished or refurbished. Back in the state pen, we'd at least had all the right tools, fasteners, and finishes needed to build or stain the cabinetry we worked on. Shovels and pikes for trench work or grave-digging detail. Heavy-duty garbage bags and trash grabbers for highway beautification. In order for me to stay on the property and be employed under Otter's general contractor's license, I had to clean out the bus and remodel the interior to make it livable, something his wife, Thrush, had wanted commissioned. He had offered me this arrangement after I was picked up for a demo cleanup job outside one of the home-improvement warehouses, where I huddled with the Mexicans and South Americans who weren't so different from me, labeled by a nation's borders and not our tribal or Indigenous identities: Maya, Otomí, Amuesha, Diné. Otter was surprised by my fluent English and knowledge of carpentry. After I had cleared the jobsite and helped hang a couple of cabinets, we worked a landscaping bid together: trench work, PVC, nine tons of pink granite and river rock, and some damn fountain-pond feature that he pissed in after the job was completed.

The bus was supposedly drivable, needed diesel and a fuel line, some fresh oil and a new filter, a coupling here or there, and a charged battery. Otter sat in his idling matte-black pickup behind the bus. We agreed Otter would rev the engine as a signal, then ease the truck against the bus, rock it out of the cinders, and push it down the hill. I was to ride steady and not turn too sharply at the base to avoid tipping the bus before making the clearing. Even without obstacles, the pitch didn't seem steep enough to offer much speed. When Otter revved the engine, it reverberated through the empty hull of the bus, a dull hum rattling loose screws and window casings. The dusty shell creaked as Otter rocked it with his truck. Volcanic earth crunched beneath the bus, and it inched toward the horizon. Sunlight reflected off the windshield, and amoebic sunspots floated across my vision. I imagined the roller coasters of youth, though I'd never ridden one, as the base approached quickly, and I yanked the steering wheel in the direction of the clearing. I stomped on the brake pedal and it fell uselessly to the floor. There was no emergency brake lever, only the aluminum frame where it had once been installed. Gripping the steering wheel, I cursed my displaced situation and crashed into the tree line.

Outside, black volcanic dust swirled and hot air blew over my skin. The bus had taken out a line of juniper and scrub oak but was undamaged. Behind it, smoke rose from beneath the hood of the truck, the steel grille bent around the railroad ties. Otter came limping down the hill along the tire tracks, peering at them as if they might tell him what had gone wrong. He was covered in dirt, caked black where it mixed with the blood on his arms and forehead.

"Should've secured the posts vertically lengthwise," he said. "Didn't think they'd get stuck on the goddamned bumper."

"Your ride is fucked," I said.

He shaded his eyes, one of which was beginning to swell shut, and spit.

"So it's good I bailed on the hill when I did. I might be worse off, dead, if I didn't."

He asked me if I was okay. I told him I was fine, aside from a headache and some bruises. After some moments considering me, then his truck, he suggested we walk the mile back to his place to grab radiator fluid and epoxy, get his ride running by nightfall. With the endorphins we'd released, it would be easy, at least he thought so.

We trudged up the hill toward Otter's place, looked out over the nearly two hundred cinder cones that humped and poked up from the earth. In the far distance, cobalt flats blended into ashen aqua cliffs, and a horizon-wide mesa collided with the sky. We knew we had underestimated our position, where we wanted to be, and gazed down at the wreck.

"It doesn't look all that bad," he said.

■ ■ ■

Otter and Thrush lived common-law in a single-story ranch house built on the high ground of a dried-up wash, hidden among juniper and cedar trees. A large solar panel powered the place, so they limited their use of the electronics they owned—radio, eighteen-volt contractor's pack of power tools, small electric Singer sewing machine that was also foot-powered—and spent their time reading, hemming, and repairing. There were no interior walls, so they had sectioned off three rooms by hanging sheets and old quilts from the exposed rafters; the ceiling was stapled with rows of silver-lined fiberglass insulation. But what stood out to me was the eastward-facing back porch, without curtains, which allowed in the first rays of the sun. Otter and Thrush rose at dawn, turned in an hour after dusk. It reminded me of my grandma's traditional Diné lifestyle, following day and seasonal cycles, keeping minimal possessions, living in a hogan without running water or electricity. The two had removed themselves from the lackluster college-tourist town life of Flagstaff to live thirty miles northeast in a "community" that was scattered on twenty- and forty-acre plots. Their neighbors were apocalypse-ready and social misfits: a roofing contractor who shot lemon drops for breakfast and lunch; a woman married to two different men, who alternated evenings of domesticity; a man who kept an army of stray dogs and who was known to take potshots if you drove too slowly past his property. And Otter and Thrush, too goth-gypsy for town.

"So you want to keep true to your parole?" Otter asked. "Heard that. Never had to go through it myself. Although I've spent nights locked up here and there, mostly minor offenses. How many years did you say you were in for?"

"I didn't," I said. "Semi-early release. If it makes any difference."

He shrugged, pulled a small, dirty cooler from beneath a salvaged wooden camp table that had been dismantled and rebuilt to fit the room, and laid out sandwich fixings while taking inventory of the kitchen. His eye was puffed angrily.

"Thrush," he yelled, "where'd I leave that goddamned bottle?"

I stacked stiff slices of bologna and cheddar between dry white bread, a similar feed to the ones provided in prison and boarding school. Places with strict schedules and punishment aimed at diminishing one's soul. Thrush appeared quietly from the bed area. She met my eyes and smiled.

"You must be the one," she said. "I hope you're quick and know what you're doing."

"I am, and I'll manage," I said.

Her nod to me was assertive, knowing, and I returned my gaze to my sorry excuse for a sandwich, admiring Otter for living with this oddly beautiful woman. She was an inch or two taller than him, nearly my height, her arms and legs long and gangly, her breasts and stomach full for her stature. She wore a hand-sewn navy blue dress with jump boots, her hair dyed black, obvious from the roots in her part and the blond fuzz of her underarms. I'd been told she was in her second trimester, and when she wasn't out walking alone or reading, she worked as a seamstress, doing alterations and making clothes for a boutique consignment shop back in town.

She noticed Otter's wounded eye immediately, brushed the blue, swollen skin with her fingertips, and rested her head on his shoulder. They whispered in this near embrace, neither showing any sign of closing or widening the distance between them. She pulled back, allowed her palm to drift down and off Otter's chest as she returned to the bed area, her attention elsewhere.

Otter exited the front door, reappeared with a dripping bottle.

"Had it stashed in the rain barrel to keep it cold," he said. "Works if you leave it overnight and retrieve it first thing, but you'd probably best drink it then."

He laughed, as if remembering all the mornings he'd regretted doing just that.

I ate and made another sandwich for later, wondering where the radiator fluid and epoxy might be kept. Otter took a long drink straight from the bottle, offered it to me, drool and whiskey dripping off his grayed, bristly chin. After a decade without, I no longer had the taste for alcohol, and declined. I got the impression it would be a while yet before we headed back to the truck, and so I watched the slow play of the juniper branches against the blue sky and wondered what real freedom might feel like.

■ ■ ■

Afternoon dimmed to dusk as we sat on the back porch facing the western edge of the reservation, the sand and limestone cliffs becoming undefined in the falling light. I thought back to shínálí asdzáá, my paternal grandmother, who was Naasht'ézhí dine'é born for Áshííhíí, and who had raised me when my parents no longer could. While I was in the clink, she sent me letters that she dictated to one of her daughters, even came to visit a couple of times during my first years inside, before she passed. I imagined she would tell me to keep better company, to handle the work and get on my way.

Otter was using a glass to down his whiskey now, small pour after small pour. He wasn't going to quit until he'd gone well past shit-faced and soiled himself in some way, which I assumed was a regularity, his glassy eyes bulbous.

"You ever love a woman and lose her?" he slurred. "Love her everything and everyplace?"

"Sure," I said, though he made no sense.

He hiccupped-burped and continued: "Before me, Thrush was with a painter, artist kind, not trade. The moody, self-obsessive type who thought he was the next hot shit. She was lonely, ignored, all that. I'd been hired to rebuild the storage room of the coffeehouse she worked at, making it bigger. I'd work late, well after she finished closing shop, so we could talk. It brightened us up, expressing and opening up to one another like that. Well, as it happens, we fucked in the storage room when it was complete. But she felt guilty, stopped talking to me, and continued to go around with that painter, all sullen and quiet as before. This was back in Louisiana."

Otter had verged on drinking himself to death after the artist and Thrush decided to move to Seattle, the scene there supposedly more fit for the guy's art. Unable to bear the thought of never seeing Thrush again, Otter drove straight through to Seattle, pissing in cups, eating bread loaves, and dissolving Benzedrine in coffee. When he reached her doorstep, he declared his love while the impotent canvas-cuddler stood by, meek and quiet. Otter and Thrush ended up out here after they found forty acres for forty thousand.

Otter kept circling back in his story to the price of the land so we returned indoors. I reminded him of the items needed to repair his truck and cleared the table of strewn sandwich parts while he stumbled through the darkness to the front door. Thrush had turned in sometime well before, so I moved quickly and quietly through the house. Outside, Otter fumbled loudly through a toolbox and extracted a radiator repair kit, a pair of rubber gloves. He pointed me toward a half-filled jug of radiator fluid, asked me to top it off with water from the rain barrel.

We walked without talking, Otter staggering freely across the soft ground, raising the bottle to his mouth mechanically. The night was cool—invigorated—new in its unfamiliar silence and blackness. At the clearing, he pulled a small flashlight from a plastic holster attached to his belt, shone it on the crashed vehicles. Shadows cast by the weak beam made them look more violently abandoned.

"If you plan on staying, you'll need a place to shit," he said. "Outhouse. You'll need to dig a pit and build one, or something like it."

"I used one at my grandma's old hogan," I said. "It's not a problem."

Otter pointed the light ahead of the bus, moved it from side to side.

"Over there looks as good as any to pop a squat. I'll mark it for you."

He stumbled toward a mess of trees, struggled with his pants while not letting go of the bottle, and pissed, first in his pants, then in spurts, until he was finally able to get his dick free of his fly. Walking back toward me, he cussed, took a long pull that killed the bottle, and retched but held it down.

"I don't sleep clothed anyhow," he said. "See you in the morning."

"What about the truck?" I asked.

He wavered in place, skin pale with drunken nausea, eyes like those of a surprised, guilty child. He babbled a mush of words. I shook my head, told him to hand me the epoxy. While he began to clumsily search his pockets, I took the flashlight from him and went to the truck, opened the hood, and stood watching as he dropped his keys, the epoxy, and an unopened half-pint, his night's finishing touch. He bent to pick up the items, face-planted into the cinders. I sat him upright, took the three things that would get the truck running, and got to work using the booze and a bit of the water–radiator fluid to clean the area around the crack. I applied the epoxy, filled the radiator, then threw what was left of the small bottle to Otter, who drank it down and passed out. I hefted and rolled him into the truck bed and drove back to his place. I cut the headlights and parked the truck near the front door, leaving Otter to sleep beneath one of the blue tarps he kept rolled up in his toolbox, and walked back to the bus to bivouac beneath the stars.

■ ■ ■

To leave shit piled, exposed, is a sign of sloth and inability. Otter had implied that much. A dog will bury its shit, paw dirt over its piss. Cats use boxes, have been rumored to operate toilets, lowering their asses and defecating, even wiping and flushing. This basic courtesy for the owner can be learned early and, with diligent tutoring, quickly. Humans, however, require a period of soiling themselves during the beginning and end of their lives that necessitates a changing, which otherwise puts our health and social grace at risk. Our potty training takes years, if only because all the sitting, wiping, and washing undermine the ways in which we prefer to spend our time. And once we learn to appreciate plumbing and the toilet, it's the fact that we shit that we attempt to hide.

I waited until the sun ascended the low tree line before making my way to the house. Once there, I found a small thermos of coffee, a stale sandwich, and a note thanking me for the truck repair, and saying that the two of them had headed into town for materials. I could get started on whatever I wanted or take the day for myself, they would return in the afternoon. The note was written in a careful, elongated cursive with correct punctuation, which I deduced wasn't of Otter's crafting. I gathered the tools I needed from what was available on the porch and took the thermos, throwing the moldy sandwich into the dried wash for the scavengers to fight over.

Sometime after midday, I had vacated the bus of vermin and dust, tightened the fasteners that weren't loose or rusted, discarded anything split or rotten, and dug a hole—ten feet deep and three feet in diameter—using a bucket attached to the end of a rope attached to a juniper. I removed the earth and rocks by climbing the rope, then hefted the dirt-filled bucket. On the final load, I dropped back in, exhausted and hungry, without the bucket and rope.

Black dust swirled down the hole, and the sun above me slid off the sky.

My legs buzzed and went numb, and I collapsed into an S shape. Eventually, footsteps crunched the cinders and I called out for help.

Thrush peered over the edge. Face shadowed by drooping hair.

"That's where the shit goes," she said.

"Guess I did too good a job."

"We will see about that." She laughed, vanishing from the top of the hole, her steps fading away. When she returned, her black silhouette held the rope in one hand.

"Bus looks good," she said. "Not nearly as good as this hole, though. So you think you can get it running sooner than later?"

"Sure. If the right parts are around. Isn't the goal to make it livable? Why did he have me dig a hole for an outhouse?" I asked.

"So that's what he told you. He's very good at making more work for himself around here that doesn't always have a purpose." She sighed heavily, tossing down the rope.

I climbed out with some effort and tried standing, but my legs wobbled and I fell on my ass.

"How long have you been down?"

"Long enough," I said, massaging the circulation back into my thighs and knees.

She helped me up, patted the dirt from my clothes. The warmth of her hands made me realize I was cold. She licked her thumb, rubbed roughly a dirt splotch near my eye like my grandma would have, and pointed to a jug of water she had brought. I choked as I gulped, got a head rush, and bent over with my head between my knees, taking deep breaths.

"Jesus Christ, you really did yourself in," she said.

"Been through worse in the actual hole. Well, this is an *actual* hole, but the hole, hole when I was locked up. Solitary."

"Otter told me a bit about that. Not anything I need to worry about, though, right?"

"No," I said. "I'm not one of those criminals. But I am one too."

"I'm not trying to pry," she said. "We're making dinner. That's why I came down. Otter's manning the fire and grill. We got everything to hopefully get the bus going. All the livability shit can wait, be done as time goes by. Let's go. I'm sure you haven't eaten all day."

I grabbed a hoodie from my pack, and we started out toward the house. She walked slowly, for my benefit, perhaps, and I was grateful, the pinpricks in my extremities softening with blood flow. We navigated the faint path by the horizon's thin line of orange and sapphire, the moon's sharp illumination. She stopped suddenly and I collided with her, inhaled the musky, patchouli scent of her body and hair. I apologized and she reached into her skirt pocket, removed a pouch of roll-your-owns, and faced me, raising her eyebrows.

"Sure," I said.

She rolled two smokes and handed me one, lit hers first, then offered me the flame. I leaned in, cupped it against the breeze, and tried not to touch her hands. It had been so long since I had touched a woman—really, another person—and I froze. She gripped my hands. I drew in the flame and moved quickly away.

"You know," she said, "that story Otter told about him and I ending up together didn't happen exactly like he told it."

"Let me guess," I said. "He never drove all that way?"

"No, he drove the whole way. But he didn't just arrive at my doorstep and sweep me off my feet. He lived in his truck for nearly six months doing odd jobs for money. It wasn't until Howie kept disappearing and our apartment slowly emptied and the tracks on Howie's arm led from one to the other, and between his fingers, that I'd even talk to Otter."

She stared into the memory, taking a long drag. I puffed my cigarette lightly.

"The fucking bullshit I've put up with from you fellas," she said. "Not *you* in particular, of course, but men. Just goddamned fucking men. I should have ditched Howie sooner, that's obvious from this perspective. And now. I've waited too long. Again."

The shadows of evening and the ember of her cigarette revealed the gaunt lines of her face. She was tired, not from anything that day or the ones before it, but from those facts recounted over and over in her head. I knew the exhaustion of nostalgia, the self-deprecating regret, and how one could mourn the present. What I didn't know was that one could eventually, under the right circumstances, make a choice, which is maybe what Thrush knew.

We reached the house and she let me enter first. No one was inside, though a few candles had been lit. Smoke drifted in through the sliding door, creating a horror-movie ambience. She grabbed cups from the cabinet, gave me one without a glance, and led the way out back.

Outside, Otter stood before a fire, used an unlit cigarette to make slight stabbing motions as he talked to himself or the fire—which one, I wasn't sure, and didn't care to know.

When he saw us, he said, "The grill's ready. You'd better be hungry. Where've you been all damn day? Are you that slow digging a hole?"

"No, I'm just sore from yesterday." I looked at Thrush, who grinned.

"He dug himself that hole you wanted and got stuck in it," she said.

Otter doubled over laughing, nearly stumbled into the fire. He was drunk again already. He called me a stupid shit, asked if I'd ever in my life dug a hole over my head. I hadn't, so I shrugged.

"I've fallen off most everything I've worked on," he said. "But I've never dug myself into a hole I couldn't get myself out of, never known anyone who has."

We all laughed then, holding our guts. It was funny—pure

accident. The only person who could be held accountable was me, for forgetting one simple thing: my way out.

■ ■ ■

Out back by the fire, Otter drank beer after beer punctuated by small sips of whiskey, which he kept poorly hidden behind a folding chair. Thrush seasoned small steaks with kosher salt, black and cayenne pepper, brushed cubed potatoes with olive oil, and topped them with fresh rosemary from her herb garden and packed them into aluminum foil packets that she placed on top of the hot coals. I wondered why she hadn't said anything about Otter's one-man party. It was obvious she knew he thought he was being sneaky with the bottle, but she appeared happy—resolute, even—and made a salad to go with the meat and potatoes. When the meal was ready, we ate without speaking, though at intervals Otter moaned loudly, smacking his lips with pleasure. I hadn't eaten so good since my grandmother's mutton stew, which she also flavored with salt, pepper, and cayenne, but added turmeric and cumin, crushed cloves of garlic, and the small, tubular wild onions she picked while herding sheep. Her family had teased her relentlessly for all the added ingredients, called her too fancy, but always gobbled up anything she made. She had been different in that way from the rest of her traditional and sometimes overly simplistic family: curious, innovative, and adaptive.

The evening was cut short when Otter began a pointless diatribe about relationships and the key to happiness. His viewpoint was that someone either walked with you, saw things your way, or walked alone. "You walk the path I give you," a sentiment similar to those of Christianity battered into our heads at school and in prison. Thrush disagreed, saying that compromise was necessary; otherwise, one just dragged the other along. Otter responded that in a compromise, no one could ever be happy, ever. Then they both turned and asked me what I thought love and compromise might be.

"I don't know," I said. "Before I got locked up, I wasn't really a stable relationship type of guy. The things I was involved in didn't bring about the best people. I'd be with a girl for a while and she'd leave, or I'd leave, and then it'd start all over again with a different person. I was a reliable, temporary fix, like epoxy."

Otter pondered my comment while sipping openly from the bottle of whiskey, before shouting, "I'll drink to that." He continued his boilermaker combination with gusto while Thrush and I collected the plates and silverware. At one point he rose to kiss Thrush, but she pushed him away, telling him how horrible he was at it when drunk. And then he shoved her. She staggered backward but kept her footing. After I was sentenced, a cousin of mine gave me the advice that I shouldn't show any signs of weakness or fear, "Don't cry or express anything like, *I don't deserve to be here.* Keep to yourself and let all those feelings die inside you." What I knew of my life was gone, far into the past. I had to be a new me for a new future, an alternate reality. My cousin and I, we'd both survived boarding school, and he said it was the same: strict routines, punishments, Christ talk everywhere you went, but a place to sleep, with three meal-like things a day. The first few months I was taunted, intimidated, and attacked. I fought back, put a guy in the infirmary, and was sent to the hole for a week, which felt like a thousand years, if a thousand years is even a thing that can be felt.

Before I could get to pummeling Otter, Thrush yanked me off him by the collar. "I can handle this," she said. "It's nothing new. He never does anything more than shove me before he breaks down. Finish cleaning up here and I'll get him inside. Trust me."

I scraped the leftovers into a separate compost bin and trash bin, wiped them clean with a wetted cloth napkin. Thrush returned about ten minutes later with Otter's keys, motioning with her head for me to follow her to the truck. Once we were both inside, she turned the ignition and revved the engine loudly.

"Asshole," she said. "I made him finish the bottle. Maybe he'll asphyxiate in his sleep. At the very least he'll have one hell of a hangover and won't get up until the afternoon. That should give us plenty of time."

"For what?" I asked.

"To finish what you started and get that bus running."

She drove along the road slowly, the black sky heavy with stars. The moon seemed to be waning, and I couldn't recall if it had been full or not the past couple of nights, the shadows between the trees the dark cobalt blue of mechanics' coveralls. When I was inside, I often dreamed of the moon, a moon I remembered seeing high above the canyon near where shínálí asdzáá had her hogan. She told me that the moon made people go crazy if you stared at it for too long. Made you desire unreachable and frivolous things. For me, it had been money and nice threads, even getting a little love from the ladies. Typical in so many ways, like my ability to dream was basic and overrated. Thrush and I sat silently with our thoughts until we reached the bus, a pink monolith in the evening darkness.

"Everything's in the truck bed," she said. "I just need the bus to get me into town. I have a guy there who really knows these things who will give it a thorough once-over before I head down to Tucson. I have a community there who will help me with the livability situation. They even know how to install solar panels and AC units."

"Time to go, I guess?"

"You saw what happened back there," said Thrush. "I can't have a baby in this godforsaken place with that useless piece of shit. Look, I've been trying for months—since I found out I was pregnant—to get this bus running. I even offered to help Otter, but he'd get so drunk that I was afraid he'd do more damage than good. I convinced him that paying someone to fix it would give him one less thing to do and that we could then turn around and sell it at a profit. I even pretended to have found a buyer."

I nodded, said, "You ever thought of getting a dog to help protect you?"

Thrush laughed. "We had one. Otter ran her over when he was blacked out, no memory of it. Thinks she ran away or got stolen, most likely stolen, because what animal would run away from him? I buried her near the front porch, under a pot of wildflowers, which he's never even noticed."

I unloaded the new battery, a set of new terminals, the fuel line and couplings, two ten-gallon fuel canisters, a case of oil and an oil filter, a case of radiator fluid and windshield cleaner, an air filter, a timing belt, and Otter's tool kit. Thrush told me she was going to gather some things from the house while I got to the repairs. In boarding school, I had excelled at three things: my automotive and fine-carpentry classes and blasphemy, which got me many days of detention, extra chore duty, and strikes from the paddle that the Father kept high on the wall above his desk. I recited so many Hail Marys and Our Fathers that I yearned for sin and the adornments it could bring. I started with the air filter—the old one was much too small, stuffed in with an old shirt to keep it in place. Next I bled the oil onto the cinders because there was no pan around and I'd never return to this place. The fuel line was easier to install than I had expected, and I took note of how clean the engine was, admiring all the maintenance Thrush had been able to do. She had planned this moment, getting the bus's engine ready by keeping it cleaned and oiled, and I thought of the many walks Otter had mentioned her taking. How oblivious he was to his own ineptitude, and now a sucker like me had been driven far out here to get all the final pieces in place. The employment required for my parole was at stake, and I began to wonder why I was helping Thrush and what of my own sense of desperation had brought me to this place. Fear. Fear of having no one left, nowhere to go, and nothing to do but fail and take the revolving door back inside. I could steal the truck and be done with all this, I thought, but theft wasn't what I went in for or what I was good at. Keeping my hands busy and moving product: that's what I'd been good at—well, until I got caught. But after that, just keeping my hands busy, my body busy. I installed the new terminals and battery, took Otter's tool kit into the bus to double-check the fasteners they had purchased so nothing could come loose once this thing started its journey back into town.

The truck bed was filled when Thrush returned, and we were both startled with something like a sonorous crack when we saw each other.

"This is everything that's essential," she said. "Which, actually, are the majority of my things. Help me get them into the bus?"

I loaded and secured the heavier items while Thrush added a couple of bags and stripped anything useful or valuable from the truck. She asked me to siphon out the gasoline. I told her that the bus was diesel, which she knew, and she told me we could potentially trade the gas or use it to douse the truck and house.

"I'm not an arsonist or murderer," I said.

"That's good," she said. "I feel like I'm getting somewhere with you. Now let's get this thing on the road."

Birds like miniature bells began to signal the rising sun. The bus sputtered and died many times before Thrush and I decided to pour a little fuel into the carburetor in order to get the diesel and air to combust. When it grumbled to life, Thrush cried out ecstatically, putting the bus into gear and sideswiping Otter's truck as she reversed and pointed us toward the way out. The uneven and gouged road jostled loose all the dust packed into the crevices of the interior, so I opened some of the side windows to release it. We hit the traffic-less paved road in a cloud of dirt and exhaust.

Thrush accelerated, the bus growled, and she shouted while pounding the steering wheeling, "Fuck you, you fucking motherfucker."

I thought of the distance I had come, though I felt I hadn't come from anywhere in that moment, that I had always just been confined to a cell or lost in the wilderness, a circulating wind thrashing up places not seen or acknowledged by human eyes, by human hands. I was heading to a place or places where human hands had continued to remake and reshape a world I wasn't used to. And seeing what I thought to be joy emanating from Thrush, a joy of new and greater possibility, I wanted to be rooted to a place or to a practice. To arrange carefully, every day, the future of my hidden existence.

Acknowledgments

I'm grateful for the support of a MacDowell fellowship and the Virginia G. Piper Fellow in Residence where I was able to re-imagine not only the future of these stories but the future of my existence. This collection took two lifetimes: so much love to the allies and good folks in those places.

Thanks to Katie Dublinski and everyone at Graywolf Press for the many reads and comments on my work, and for helping me make this collection a reality.

To the teachers whom I apprenticed with at Northern Arizona University, Arizona State University, and the Prague Summer Program, much respect and many thanks for pushing me and holding me to high standards: Jim Simmerman, Allen Woodman, Ann Cummins, Jane Armstrong, Jeff Berglund, Melissa Pritchard,

Alberto Ríos, Anjana Appachana, T. M. McNally, Simon Ortiz, Cynthia Hogue, and Stuart Dybek.

To my friends, readers, editors, and fellow writers: Matt Bell, Fernando Peréz, Shomit Barua, Mark and Kelly Haunschild, Daniel Salcido, Metal Joe, Bryan Stewart, Tiffany Midge, Christian Perticone, Sarah Hynes, Kenny Redner, Travis Franks, Eric and Erin Aldrich, Beth Staples, Anna Lena Phillips Bell, Ron Spatz, Douglas Glover, Katie Berta, Kent Corbin, Irvin Morris, Elijah Tubbs, Kennedy Dawn Sterns, Izzy Montoya, Adrienne Celt, Dave Clark, Ruben Cu:k Ba'ak, Sherwin Bitsui, Bill Wetzel, Brendan Basham, and Roland Jackson.

To my colleagues at the University of Arizona for scooping me out of the sludge: Ander Monson, Manuel Muñoz, Aurelie Sheehan, Kate Bernheimer, Farid Matuk, and Susan Briante. And to the students who always wow the hell out of me.

To shimá dóó shizhe'é dóó shideizhí dóó shidine'é. For every goddamned beautiful thing. To my brother Kumen, and all his family. To my sister Raquel, and all her family.

And, most important, Sara Sams and Billie Dólii, for love and light.

Bojan Louis is Diné of the Naakai dine'é, born for the Áshįįhí. He is the author of a book of poetry, *Currents*, which received an American Book Award. He has been a resident at MacDowell. He teaches creative writing at the University of Arizona.